Love Intolerant
By: Jessica Terry

I0629826

LOVE INTOLERANT

First edition. March 12, 2023.

ISBN: 979-8988003601

Written by Jessica Terry.

Dedication

I started this book several years ago based off a general idea of writing about a "regular" woman, though I had no set storyline in mind. I wrote the first chapter and the first couple of paragraphs of the second, and then it went on the shelf for a *long* while as I worked on other things.

Then out of the blue, the story hit me and the age gap romance began to take form. It became my 2021 NaNoWriMo project and I fell completely and totally in love with it. And now it's finally its turn for y'all to (hopefully) enjoy.

I'm super thankful for everybody who showed support by letting me bounce ideas off of them or ask them random research questions or letting me use their embarrassing stories for my books (and telling me to go to bed when I'm up until the wee hours writing). My amazing son Langston, my mother Barbara, sister Jennifer, brother-in-law Tony, neices Lace and Alex, and my father Alton, who is no longer with us on earth but is forever in my heart and mind; Desmond, who is always 'Team Jessica' and shows me unlimited support and encouragement without me even having to ask...my friends, church family, fellow authors, readers, anyone who shares my content...I take nothing for granted and appreciate you ALL more than you know.

Chapter 1

I WONDERED IF HE COULD smell the cheesecake on my breath as he hugged me goodnight.

"I had a nice time," Bradley mumbled politely as he hugged my thick-ish waist. Classic church hug; our bodies were barely touching.

"Me, too," I replied just as politely. My hand gave his shoulder an obligatory pat. "Thank you for dinner."

"No problem." He released me and stepped back, smiling tightly. He quickly glanced at his watch, looking somewhat awkward as if he had no idea how to go ahead and end this miserable excuse for a date we were on. "Umm..."

"Well, get home safe, Bradley," I spoke up, putting him out of his misery. I was just as anxious to leave as he was. "And take care of yourself."

Looking relieved, Bradley nodded. "You too, Adele. You, um, you want me to walk you back to your car?"

"If you want to," I replied with a shrug. Looking at him over the rim of my glasses, I smirked knowingly. "But I know you really don't, do you? You can go ahead and admit it."

Bradley looked surprised at my candor, then chuckled. Some of the tension was already melting from his shoulders. "I wouldn't say I don't *want* to..."

"But you can't wait to get to your car so you can get the hell out of here, right?"

He actually blushed. Kinda cute. "Wow."

"I keep it real, sweetheart," I informed him, brushing some of my reddish-brown locs out of my face. "You and I both know nothing is happening here. This date sucked. I've had colonoscopies more comfortable than this."

Throwing his head back, Bradley's loud laughter filled the parking garage we were standing in. He then gave me his first genuine smile of the evening as he stepped closer to me. "I'm glad to know it's not just me that wasn't really feeling it."

"Not at all."

"Don't get me wrong; you're cool, but-"

"You don't have to do that," I interjected, giving a dismissive wave. "One thing I'm not lacking in is self-esteem. You don't have to worry about bruising my ego."

Bradley smiled at me again, nodding slowly. "I respect that," he mused appreciatively. I saw his toffee brown eyes roam over my body again, as if looking at it in a new light. Even though I could see the slight disappointment in his eyes when we first met up on this blind date, it suddenly seemed they liked what they saw now. I guess me being such a hoot was adding to my appeal.

"I'll be sure to let Rashida know how this turned out so she won't try this with anybody else," I joked, though I meant it. Rashida was my friend and the facilitator of this total waste of an outfit. Bradley was cute and seemed like a nice guy, but I knew when a man was attracted to me and when he wasn't. And he wasn't; it was written all over his face when he saw me. "Make her reimburse you for the evening."

Laughing again, Bradley shortened the distance between us even more. He didn't seem to be in a hurry to leave like he had been a couple of minutes before.

"It wasn't all that bad," he insisted, touching my arm. "I wouldn't mind hanging out with you again, actually."

"Yeah? Well, that's nice of you to say."

"I'm not just saying it, though. I mean it, Adele."

"Mmm-hmm," I grunted with a smile. He hadn't wanted to hang with me before I called this date out for what it was. But I didn't take offense; us not being compatible wasn't anybody's fault. "All right, then. Well, you have my number, if you ever want to use it."

"Absolutely."

"Well, I'm gonna head on home," I announced, fishing my phone out of my purse and glancing at the time. It wasn't even nine o'clock.

"You sure? We could go get some coffee or something..."

"I'm good on the coffee. Trying to cut back. Plus, I only have a little while before I start to embarrass myself."

Bradley looked at me, confused. "What do you mean, embarrass yourself? Embarrass yourself how?"

"In about another half hour or so I'll be a gurgling, gassy mess from that cheesecake. I'm defiantly lactose intolerant."

This, too, was hilarious to Bradley and he cracked up like I was on stage at Def Comedy Jam. It was the absolute truth, though, and I knew he wouldn't be laughing when he heard me start rumbling and farting like an old Chevy.

"Let me go ahead and walk you to your car, then," he offered with a smile, taking me by the elbow.

"Hold up..." I stopped walking, grabbing his arm for support as I reached down to take off my peep-toed pumps. They had been pinching my feet and I was done trying to be cute for the evening. I sighed contently as I wiggled my pedicured toes in relief. "That's better."

"You're just gonna walk across this pavement barefoot?" Bradley marveled as he walked alongside me.

I shrugged. "Either that, or you'll be carrying me to my car. And I don't really remember where I parked. I'm not trying to be blamed for causing premature back problems 'cause you were toting me around this parking lot."

"Girl…" Bradley chuckled again, shaking his head. He was really getting a kick out of me now.

We made comfortable conversation as we tried to find my car in the Atlantic Station parking deck, talking about things we hadn't bothered trying to talk about during dinner. I learned he was an only child, had a young daughter, owned a tow truck company, and he hated blueberries. I don't even know how that one came up.

"There it is!" I exclaimed, pointing to my blue Nissan in relief.

"You sure?"

I pressed the 'Lock' button on my key fob to make sure and was relieved when the lights flashed in confirmation. "Yep, that's it."

"Okay, then," Bradley hedged, turning to me. "I really would love to hang out with you again, Adele."

I smiled. He really was cute. Too bad I was probably firmly locked in the friend zone already to him. But it wasn't anything I wasn't used to. "Like I said, you have my number. We'll see if you use it."

"Oh, I definitely will." He held his arms out for a hug and when I stepped into them, he held me much closer than he had during our earlier hug. His hands actually roamed my back a little bit instead of being glued to my waist. Even kissed my cheek. "Let me know when you make it home, all right?"

"Will do," I winked at him before getting into my car and starting the engine. Bradley stood there and watched as I pulled out of the parking space, then waved as I drove off. I chuckled to myself as I shook my head. Not as disastrous as it initially looked like it would turn out, but I wouldn't exactly call the date a win, either. I doubted there would ever be any romance between me and Bradley.

I was about ten minutes from my house when Rashida called. I knew she probably couldn't wait to get the run-down on how everything went. Pressing the button on the steering wheel to answer the call, I braced myself for the barrage of questions. "Hello?"

"How'd it go?" Rashida asked excitedly. "You aren't still with him, are you? If so just hang up and call me back; you don't even have to respond."

She was funny. "I'm almost home, girl."

"Is Bradley following you there?"

"Why would he be following me there?"

"So you can continue the evening at your place, of course."

"Nah...that's not happening."

"Why not? You two didn't hit it off?"

"Not 'til we got to the parking lot, we didn't."

"What happened in the parking lot? *Ooh*, did you two start making out up against the car and get so hot and heavy that you forgot where you were? Did you grind-"

"Let me stop you right there, girl," I cut her off before she started spelling out a Zane-worthy sex scene. "Nothing even *close* to that happened. All I meant was that once I made it clear that I was as aware of how bad the date had gone as he was, we both relaxed and were more at ease with each other, that's all."

"Aww, hell," Rashida grunted. "That's it?"

"What did you expect? For us to fall madly in love and elope?"

"Well, no, but I certainly expected for you to do better than not getting along until it was time to leave."

"Yeah, well. That's how it went." I steered the car into my driveway and parked, leaving the engine running. I ran a hand through my locs and sighed.

"Adele," Rashida's voice was a stern/concerned mix as it filled my car through the Bluetooth. "What *really* happened?"

I knew what she was asking. "He saw me, and...wasn't feeling me. I could see it all over his face."

"Oh, Adele..."

I shrugged. "Not a big deal. To his credit, he was at least polite about it."

"I'm so sorry."

"For what?"

"I'm the one that bugged you about going out with him. I know you don't really like blind dates..."

"You don't have to apologize to me for anything. These things happen."

"But they shouldn't keep happening to *you*," Rashida insisted. "It shouldn't be this hard for you to meet somebody. You're an amazing woman."

"Thank you for the compliment. But I'm apparently not what most men want; at least, the ones I've met. They need to be physically attracted, too, and, for the most part, I just don't do it for them like that."

"Don't say that."

"Rashida, I'm not being self-deprecating, here. I'm secure in how I am. But I also don't hold any delusions about myself, either...most men just don't go for regular chicks like me."

"You are not *regular*."

"You know what I mean."

"I actually don't."

"Yes, you do. You just don't want to say it. It's cool, though."

"Adele, you talk as if you're not cute."

"I'm adorable," I concurred, smiling. "But I'm plain. And my body is like mashed potatoes."

"Stop that."

"Pot roast?"

"Adele!" Rashida was damn near hollering at me. "There is nothing wrong with your body!"

I giggled. "I was just playing, girl, chill out."

"It wasn't funny. Say something *positive* about your body, for once."

"Hey, *I'm* fine with my lusciousness as it is. But it doesn't turn heads like yours does."

"I don't know what you're talking about. I don't get any more attention than you do."

"So we're lying now, huh?" I chuckled, getting my phone from my purse to put to my ear as I finally turned the car engine off. I stepped out of the car, slinging my purse over my shoulder and grabbing my shoes from the front seat. "Didn't you have a date tonight, yourself? How did that go?"

"Oh, um..." Rashida hedged. I shook my head, smiling.

"If it went well, you can say so," I informed her as I unlocked the front door to my house. "It's not gonna hurt my feelings."

"He's...kinda still here."

"What are you on the phone with me for, then? Get back to your date; we can talk tomorrow."

"Girl, it's fine. He's asleep, anyway."

"Wore him out, huh?" I laughed. Rashida giggled as confirmation. "I'm home, anyway, and I need to check on this boy. Plus, my stomach is starting to act up."

"Oh, no. What did you eat?"

Laughing, I headed up the stairs to my bedroom. Rashida knew me too well. I could hear the music coming from my son's room as I passed it. "Cheesecake."

"Why do you do that to yourself? You know good and well you're lactose intolerant."

"I wanted it so I had it," I shrugged.

"You *do* know there are plenty of dairy-free alternatives that are just as good, right?"

"No they're not."

"How do you know, Adele? Have you tried them all?"

"I've tried enough. And you know my policy on fake dairy. It's either the real deal or nothing."

"Ugh."

"Anyway. I could eat whatever I wanted tonight 'cause it's not like I had to worry about trying to impress Bradley, since I already knew he wasn't interested. Plus, I knew the date would be over by the time the effects would kick in."

"I don't even know what to do with you sometimes," Rashida muttered. "All right, then. Kiss my godbaby for me and call me tomorrow."

"Will do. Love you."

"Love you, too."

I took a moment to send a quick text to Bradley letting him know I was home before I opened the door to my bedroom, tossed my purse on my bed and my shoes on the floor, then padded back to Christopher, my sixteen-year-old son's room. I knocked one needless time before poking my head in. As usual, he was glued to that damn cell phone.

When he saw me, he sat up and laid his phone down next to him on the bed. "Hey, Ma. How was your date?"

"Ehh," I shrugged, entering the room and dropping onto the foot of his bed with my leg tucked under me. "Nothing to write home about."

"Another one bites the dust, huh?"

"It went all right."

"I'm sorry, Ma."

"Nothing for you to be sorry for," I shrugged again. I'd made it a policy to never whine and complain about my dates to my son. "It is what it is."

"You'll find somebody."

"I know."

"Is that a new dress?"

"I've worn this dress a hundred times, Christopher."

"Really?"

"Lord, have mercy," I shook my head, smiling. "You're getting too old not to be more observant than that."

"Oh, I'm *very* observant," Christopher assured me, unfolding his long legs. He had hit his growth spurt over the summer and now towered over me. "I observe *plenty*."

"Uh-huh. I bet you do."

"Can I bring somebody by here tomorrow?"

"Who?"

"Nikki."

"Who is Nikki? Your girlfriend or something?"

"If she acts right." He smirked.

His cocky ass. These little girls running up behind him had his head the size of Georgia. "Whatever. Yeah, you can bring her when I get home. Just remember what we talked about."

"I know, Ma. I don't want kids no more than you want grandkids. I haven't had any sex or anything."

"Glad to hear it but more than that, I've told you to always be honest with girls and not try be some kind of player," I emphasized, my eyes serious. "If you're not interested in them, don't let them think you are."

"I won't."

"And don't be walking around here like you're king of the hill, either. Don't let these lil' girls blow your head up. Your doo-doo stinks just like everybody else's."

As if on cue, my stomach gurgled loudly. I placed a hand over my belly and turned sheepish eyes to my son.

"Ma...what did you eat? Some ice cream or something?"

"Cheesecake."

"Cheesecake? You know you're not supposed to be eating any cheesecake. Now you're gonna be in the bathroom all night."

"Oh well," I grinned, standing. "It was worth it."

Christopher just shook his head.

I held my locs away from my face as I leaned down to give him a double kiss on the forehead. "That's from me and your Auntie Rashida. Don't stay up too late, now."

"Yes, ma'am."

I turned and headed towards the door, my hand still on my stomach. I could feel him looking at me and waited for what I knew was coming.

"I love you, Ma," he said to my back. I smiled. For whatever reason, ever since he hit puberty he was too shy to tell me he loved me to my face. But at least he still said it.

"Love you too, baby," I replied without turning around. My stomach gurgled again and I picked up the pace towards my bathroom, picking up the latest copy of *Essence* from my nightstand to keep me company.

Chapter 2

"WHERE YOU BEEN? THE gym?" Dad asked me.

"Yes, sir." I cleaned my glasses with the hem of my t-shirt before sliding them back onto my face. "Figured I'd stop by and see you before I went home."

"It's always good to see you," he replied, giving me his usual half-smile. "I'm glad you started knocking, though, instead of just using your key."

"One time seeing you in your underwear is quite enough."

"Well, hell. It's *my* house." Dad shrugged as he sat up to retrieve his whiskey from the coffee table. "I can wear whatever I want to."

"I'm not disagreeing."

"What did you go to the gym for? I thought you were on some kind of crusade to stay fat."

I chuckled. Most people might have taken offense to this kind of statement, but I knew how to deal with my father. Stuart Dobbs was a very blunt and straightforward man; he didn't hold his tongue about anything. Well, almost anything. "It's not a *crusade*...I like to take care of myself. I'm just not fanatical about working out like a lot of people are. And I'm not fat."

"You're a little jiggly."

"I'll accept jiggly. In some areas."

"So what you workin' out for, then?"

"To avoid getting to fat."

We shared a laugh at that.

I liked hanging out with Dad; I guess you could say we'd become friends once I hit adulthood. Our relationship had been okay before that, but he used to be a lot more gruff and stern back in the day. He softened up a lot after Mama died. Losing a spouse could do that. I would know.

Damn shame that was the main thing we had in common.

"How's that boy doin'?" Dad asked, referring to Christopher.

"Just fine. Growing like a weed and eating up all the damn snacks as soon as I buy 'em."

"Maybe he ain't just *growing* like a weed but *smokin'* some, too."

"I doubt it but if he is, he's doing an excellent job of hiding it so far. I think he's just greedy as hell."

"If you say so."

"Matter of fact, I'm gonna need to be getting back to the house in a little bit," I realized, checking the time on my phone. "He wants to bring his lil' girlfriend over today and I need to get dinner started. You need me to do anything?"

"Pour some more whiskey in here."

I chuckled as I took the glass he was holding out and went over to refresh his drink. Dad had been drinking whiskey ever since I could remember. Not beer, not cognac, not anything else; just whiskey, and always Jim Beam. I didn't get the appeal because I never cared for it. It's what I imagined bull urine would taste like.

"So you ain't tired of being by yourself yet?" he asked me as I handed him his nasty alcohol back. "It's been a few years since Nate died; what, you celibate now or somethin'?"

"Not even close."

"You datin'?"

"I go on dates."

"So why don't you have a man yet?"

"It doesn't just happen, Dad. I have to meet the right one first."

"Hmph. I hope you ain't like these ladies I hear about that got a wish list a mile long of stuff they want a man to have. No one man would have all of it unless you built him in a lab. You being picky like that?"

"No, Dad. I'm not *picky* but I'm not desperate, either. No rush. And for the record, there's nothing wrong with having standards."

"I ain't saying just go with anybody; you deserve better than that. Was just makin' sure you weren't out here looking for perfection."

"No sense in looking for something I can't give in return, is it?"

Dad eyed me and I wondered if he thought I was trying to feel sorry for myself. I wasn't; just stating facts. I had made peace with my seemingly-underwhelming looks years ago. Hell, *I* thought I was cute. God made me how He wanted me to be and I was fine with it. And it had been good enough to snag a husband one time.

And *nobody* could tell me I didn't have a nice rack.

"Well, Dad, I'm gonna head home," I announced, leaning down to kiss his forehead. "I'll give you a call tomorrow."

Before he could respond, there was a knock on the door. Dad sighed and shook his head, taking a slow sip of his whiskey and leaning his head against the back of his chair.

I glanced towards the door curiously, then back at him. "Want me to get that?"

"Nah. They'll go away in a minute if we shut up."

"You know who it is?" I persisted, lowering my voice. "Why don't you wanna answer the door?"

"It's probably another one of them women bringing me another meat loaf or pie or casserole. Every damn day it's something else. My freezer can't hold no more. We didn't get that much food at your mama's wake."

"So tell 'em to stop bringing it."

"No kiddin'? That's all I gotta do?" He rolled his eyes, leaning forward to return his glass to the coffee table.

"Dad, ever since you moved over to this neighborhood you've had these women running behind you. You aren't interested in any of 'em?"

He shrugged. "Never been one for eager women. And I'm not in the mood to deal with any of those ladies right now. They'll get the hint in a minute."

Sure enough, the knocking stopped a few moments later. I went over and peeked through the curtain covering the front window and saw an older woman with a skirt that was straining over her ample behind heading back down the driveway, her pumps clicking against the pavement. She was holding what looked like a cake plate in her hands.

"Coast is clear," I informed him, moving over to the door. "Let me know if you change your mind and decide to run off and get married somewhere. I don't really *want* a new mommy at my age but-"

"Shut up and get out."

I laughed and walked outside, glad that I could find it funny that my seventy-year-old dad was getting more play than I was.

CHRISTOPHER AND HIS little girlfriend were sitting outside when I pulled up to the house. I thought I'd have a little more time before she came by, but they apparently were more eager than I expected.

My boy stood and headed over to me when I opened my car door, and girlfriend was right on his heels. This might've been a little unfair, but she was already on my nerves just for that.

"Hey, Ma," Christopher greeted me, grabbing my workout bag from me as I got out of the car. "I didn't know you were going to the gym today."

"Spur of the moment decision." I accepted his kiss on the cheek and gave a quick scan to his visitor, who was holding on to his arm and grinning at me excitedly. Lord, I didn't have the energy for this. "How long have y'all been out here?"

"Not all that long, Ms. Mozley," the girl piped up before Christopher could answer. "Chris-boo told me to wait until five before I came but I went ahead and had my brother bring me on over, because I missed him and didn't want to wait. But he said we had to sit outside until you got home, which was just fine with me because it's such a nice day, and plus I *totally* respect your house rules. We even made a game out of counting how many green cars went by."

Oh my. I could tell already.

And what the hell is a Chris-boo?

Christopher was looking at me sheepishly, either silently begging me not to embarrass him or kicking himself for inviting this chatterbox over here. I couldn't tell which.

"It's nice to meet you," I made myself say politely, holding my hand out. "You must be Nikki."

"Who?"

"Oh, uh, Ma," Christopher quickly spoke up, stepping in front of...whoever this was. "I forgot to tell you...Nikki ain't comin'. This is Deena."

"Deena, huh?" I arched a brow at him. "I see. Well, Deena, it's nice to meet *you*."

"You too, Ms. Mozley." Deena smiled, apparently unfazed by being mistaken for someone else by the boy she was supposed to be going with. "Chris-boo is always talking about what a cool mama he has. Is that your natural hair color?"

"Nah, I let Dark and Lovely help me out with this. Let's go on in the house; you two hungry? I'm gonna get dinner started."

"Oooh, what are we having? Just so you know, I don't eat pork, tomatoes, beans, or tree nuts," Deena informed me as we filed through the front door. "Other than that, I'm up for anything!"

"Good to know. I'll just save the three-bean pig feet chili with toasted almonds for tomorrow."

"Hahaaaaa!" she shrieked in laughter, playfully hitting my arm. "That is too funny! Chris-boo was right about you!"

"It's my gift. Look here, why don't y'all hang out in the living room or something while I get things going in the kitchen."

"Oh no, we can stay in here and keep you company," Deena insisted, following me. She looked back at Christopher, who was trudging behind. "Right, Chris-boo?"

"Actually, Ma likes to be by herself in the kitchen," Christopher quickly objected, reading the look I shot him. "We'd just get in her way. We can watch a movie or something while she cooks."

"Okay. That means we can cuddle, too!"

I whirled around as Deena pulled Christopher towards the couch in the living room. He shook his head slightly at me as she led him away.

Now, I wasn't one of those mothers who automatically disliked every girl her son brought home. Christopher was growing up, he was tall and handsome and all that, and I had enough sense to know that he would attract attention. But this Deena girl...I wasn't a fan. She seemed nice enough and was admittedly adorable, with her big bright eyes and her dimples and her cute little two-buns hairdo. I just wasn't sure I liked how much she was already hanging all over him like she was.

And she talked a *lot*.

I went about fixing a dinner of air-fried chicken, dirty rice, and some vegetable medley that I was sick of seeing in my freezer. Since Christopher was a bread fanatic, I threw in some Texas toast with garlic butter. And of course, I was making frequent peeks out to the living room to make sure my son and his girlfriend weren't getting too *comfortable*.

"This smells *so* good!" Deena exclaimed once I called them in to eat. She held Christopher's hand as she surveyed the table with a grin. "My stomach is growling already!"

"Well, let's go ahead and eat so we can shut that thing up, huh?" I suggested, pulling out my chair.

Deena busted out laughing. "There you go *again*! I sure wish my mama was as funny as you, Ms. Mozley!"

I just smiled and winked at her as I spread a napkin over my lap.

Deena took her seat as Christopher got the two of them some juice from the refrigerator. After we prayed and dug in, I tried to make an effort to get to know Deena better. I figured she must be all right if my boy liked her. And I made myself ignore how close she had pulled her chair to his.

"So Deena, are you and Christopher in any of the same classes?"

"No, ma'am. I'm just a sophomore; Chris-boo is a year ahead of me. We met at a football game."

"Ohh. Well, that's nice. What do you like to do?"

"You mean besides making cute little posts to send to my Chris-boo?"

It was *so* hard not to roll my eyes at that. I mean, really. I deserved an award for restraint.

"Um, yeah. Besides that."

"I'm on the dance team at school. And the yearbook committee. My brother said that stuff will look good on college applications. But if you're talking about more fun stuff, karaoke is my *jam*. And I'm learning how to make t-shirts so I can start my own little business; people love cute t-shirts."

"Right..."

"And I like to draw."

"Yeah?" I perked up. "I like to draw, too. I'm not very good at it, though. It's mostly just for stress relief."

"I bet you're not that bad. You should post them online. Sell 'em."

"Oh, no. I have a personal policy to not knowingly do anything to humiliate myself. Nobody wants to see those things. What do you like to do your drawings with? I just use pencils."

"I'm all about the crayons with mine."

When I saw she wasn't joking, I eased my eyes over to Christopher, whose butterscotch skin was turning red from trying to keep a straight face. My boy sure knew how to pick 'em.

"Nice..." I took a long sip of my ice water.

We all continued to eat in relative silence. That is, until Deena started to fill that silence with the breakdown of the music video of some rapper I'd never heard of. I noticed Christopher was barely saying anything, and I had to wonder how much he really liked this girl. He was either acting bashful with her around me or he was ready for her to go home.

"So Deena," I said, putting down my fork. "Did Christopher tell you about his ten-year plan yet?"

"Ten-year plan?"

"Uh-huh. About how he's gonna go to college, major in Farm Management and-"

"Did you say *Farm Management*?"

"Oh, you didn't know he was into agriculture? Yes, girl, he's already started saving to buy some prime land somewhere away from the city and start his own business selling those crops. So whoever he ends up with will need to be cool with farm livin'. Bonus points if she can drive a tractor." I looked at Christopher. "Right, baby?"

"Sure," Christopher concurred from behind the napkin he was pretending to wipe his mouth with.

"Oh," Deena croaked, draining the rest of her juice and putting down her glass. "That's um...cool." She glanced at Christopher, then pulled her phone from her pocket and looked at the screen. "Aww man...I didn't realize what time it was. I have a bunch of chores and stuff to do at home. I'd better call my brother to come get me."

"I *totally* get that," I assured her. "Go ahead and call. We wouldn't want you to get in trouble. Christopher has some stuff he needs to do tonight, himself."

"Okay, I'll tell my brother to hurry up, then." Deena shot out of her chair and hurried to the living room with her phone pressed to her ear. Christopher just raked his fork through his second serving of dirty rice, shaking his head. I still couldn't tell whether he was pleased or upset about what I told Deena.

Deena's brother must have been nearby because he was honking the horn from outside barely ten minutes later.

"Thanks for dinner, Ms. Mozley," Deena said, inching towards the door. Christopher and I had walked her to the living room. "It was really, really yummy."

"I'm so glad."

"And Christopher...I'll see you at school tomorrow."

What happened to Chris-boo?

And with that, she hurried out the door.

After locking the door behind her, Christopher turned to me. "Farm Management, Ma?"

"It's an honorable major."

"I don't wanna major in that."

"I know you don't. But I figured that was something she wouldn't want any part of."

"So you lied."

"Yeah, I lied. Don't think that's something *you* should do, though. This is one of those 'do as I say not as I do' situations."

"So you didn't like her, I guess."

"Never mind if *I* liked her or not. Did *you*? You were barely saying anything the whole time she was here. That's not really like you."

"She's all right." He went over and plopped onto the couch. "But she's kinda clingy. I didn't realize that at first. Not to mention, I hate that stupid nickname she gave me."

Chuckling, I went and joined him on the couch. "It was more of a pet name, son. And yeah, it was kinda silly but that's what you do when you really like somebody. I used to call your dad Snuggle Hunk."

"Wow, Ma. I'm glad I never heard that."

"Whatever. What I want to know, though, is how Deena was here when it was Nikki that you asked for permission to bring over. What happened to her?"

"Some new guy transferred to our school from out of state and a bunch of the girls went crazy over him since he's supposed to be real big-time in basketball. Nikki went to the movies with him."

"So Deena was the rebound?"

"I wouldn't say that. She's been eyeing me for a while and I always thought she was cool so I figured I should try to get to know her. And she's nice. But I don't want a girlfriend that talks that much. She doesn't even seem to notice when I don't say anything back."

Laughing, I fell against the back of the couch. I had to take off my glasses and wipe my eyes, it cracked me up that much. Christopher chuckled at me.

"You know I'm gonna have to set her straight about what I'm gonna major in, right?" he informed me after he had turned on the television. "I don't want her going around thinking I'm planning on majoring in Farm Management."

"Well son, I hate to break it to ya, but she's probably already told somebody about that, as chatty as she is."

"Ugh. Thanks a lot, Ma. Though I *do* appreciate you getting her out of here 'cause I was ready for her to go home, anyway."

"I kinda figured."

"I'll just tell her I changed my mind. Or not. Whatever. I don't care what she thinks one way or the other. Do we have any of that pound cake left?"

We spent the rest of the evening hanging out together; cleaning up the kitchen, eating cake and watching *Ridiculousness*. It was during this that Christopher suggested some ridiculousness of his own.

"Ma, why don't you join a dating site?"

Scoffing, I set my crumbs-littered plate on the coffee table and stretched my arms over my head. "Yeah, right."

"What's wrong with that? I saw a commercial for that dating site for old people."

"I'm only forty-five. I don't think that applies to me yet."

"Well, still. There's plenty of other ones."

"Baby, I appreciate the suggestion but I'm all right. I'm not in any hurry. I'll meet a nice man when I'm meant to."

He eyed me with a glint of skepticism, but thankfully left it alone. I meant what I said about not being in a hurry, but it wasn't lost on me that both my dad *and* my son had more luck with the opposite sex than I did.

Chapter 3

"WELL, I'LL BE DAMNED..."

I saw the text from Bradley come in while I was at work but couldn't check it right away. I'd almost forgotten about him; our blind date had been close to a month earlier. Maybe he *hadn't* just been blowing smoke when he said he wanted to hang out again.

Stuffing my phone into my pocket, I put the text out of my mind while I went on about my work. I'd been the Activities Director at Westwood Oaks, an assisted living facility, for several years and it might not have been the sexiest job but I enjoyed it. I'd much rather work around the elderly than a bunch of kids any day of the week (though I did love kids).

Even though I was only halfway through the schedules I was supposed to have finished by the end of the day, I decided to take a few minutes and go see my favorite resident, Ms. Corine. I loved visiting her because she was always in such good spirits and was almost always an instant pick-me-up. Plus, she was entertaining as hell. She actually didn't mind being in the facility, unlike most of the residents; she said it was nice to have people doing all the cooking and cleaning that she'd been doing for herself for years.

"I was wondering if you were gonna have time to come by and see me today," Ms. Corine greeted me when I entered her room. She was a tiny little thing, barely five feet tall, and was almost dwarfed by the huge blanket she had wrapped around her shoulders. As usual, she was sitting in the chair by her bed, crocheting. All she ever ended up with were big squares because she never tried to actually learn how to follow a pattern; the activity was just relaxing to her.

"You know I always come by and bug you whenever I can." I leaned down to give her a light hug before grabbing the folding chair by the closet and taking a seat near her. "What's going on with you today?"

"Got another letter from my boyfriend. He said he'd come get me out of here just as soon as he was finished shooting this action movie he's in. I told him to make sure there are plenty of scenes where they show the tattoo with my name in it."

Another thing about Ms. Corine; she had a little bit of an imagination on her. She wasn't nuts (they had her tested); she just liked to entertain herself by making up stuff. I figured as long as she didn't actually start believing what she made up, there was no harm in it.

"Well, how 'bout that," I responded, as if she'd just told me the Braves won. "Did you eat, Ms. Corine?"

"Yeah, I ate. Even though whoever they got in that kitchen don't seem to know the first thing about salt."

"You *do* remember your high blood pressure, right? You're on a low-sodium diet."

"Oh, poo. I done made it to be this old, I should be able to eat whatever I want."

I just shook my head. She steadily fussed about the food but always ate damn near most of it.

"Well, maybe one day I'll bring you some fried chicken or something. With some biscuits, mashed potatoes, greens-"

"If you're gonna bring all that, bring some sweet potato pie, too," Ms. Corine requested. "Nothing like some good sweet potato pie."

"You got it." I could promise stuff like this because I knew she wouldn't remember. Before the night was over with, she wouldn't even be thinking about anything I said.

I hung out with Ms. Corine for a while before going back to my office. Could've stayed a little longer, but she started asking me why I didn't have a husband or a boyfriend, and the inevitable stories of how her and her late husband Charles met. Why people acted like a forty-five year old woman being single and fine with it was so puzzling, I'd never understand.

I wasn't against relationships at all. At times, I really missed being with someone like that. But really, nowadays, it was just easier to stay by myself than try to navigate the dating scene.

Despite that fact, I returned Bradley's text when I got back to my office. All his message said was to 'hit him up when I got a chance', so I figured this was just some obligatory thing that he felt he had to do since he had verbally committed to calling me after our date.

I figured I'd keep my response simple, you know; not make it seem like I was expecting anything.

ADELE: *Hey, nice to hear from you.*

He wasted no time responding, to my mild surprise.

BRADLEY: Told you I'd reach out. You've been doing all right?

ADELE*: Can't complain.*

BRADLEY: Glad to hear it. You want to meet up? Maybe go get some dinner later or something?

So he was actually asking me out. Wasn't expecting *that*.

ADELE: *That should work. Just gotta make sure my son is squared away.*

BRADLEY: No doubt. Just let me know. I should be good to go around seven, if that works for you.

ADELE: *It should. But I'll definitely get back to you when I'm sure.*

BRADLEY: Looking forward to it. It'll be good to see you again.

ADELE: *Aww, you.* ☺

I already knew I'd likely be meeting Bradley. Christopher would be fine by himself for a couple of hours.

After I got off work, I headed home so I could get something together for dinner real quick for Christopher, then get showered and changed to meet Bradley. Since I had made the mistake of telling Rashida that I was seeing Bradley again, she insisted on coming over to help me find something to wear like we were fifteen years old or something. She was acting like this was a way bigger deal than it was.

"Wear something that shows off your boobs," she advised, digging through my closet. "Men love that."

"I'm not gonna do that, Rashida."

"I don't see why not. If I had a rack like yours, I'd be showing them off every day."

"You *do* show them off every day. Just about every shirt and dress you have is low-cut."

"Whatever. We're talking about *you* right now." She emerged from my closet with a dress in each hand, neither of which I would be wearing. Of course she had managed to find the most revealing things I owned. "Bradley will love you in either one of these."

"Girl," I shook my head as I went and took the dresses from her so I could hang them back up. "I don't know what you think this is, but it's not a date like *that*. We're just going to dinner. Hanging out, you know."

"Who says? How do you know that?"

"Remember when I said that I could tell he wasn't attracted to me?"

"Well, clearly you were wrong, since he asked you out again."

"Again, it's just dinner. It's nothing romantic."

"And *again*, you don't know that." She brushed her brow-skimming bangs from her face and plopped onto my bed. "For all you know, he's realized that he likes you more than he thought he did. Otherwise, he could have very well just gone on about his business without another word."

I considered her words for a minute before shaking them off. "I doubt it."

"Why do you do that?" Rashida demanded, sitting forward and looking at me intently, her light brown eyes darkening with annoyance. "Why do you always try to downplay anything that involves a man being interested in you? The coy game isn't cute, girl."

"I'm not being coy."

"Then what is it? Because I *know* it's not that you don't think anybody would want you. I know you have more self-esteem than that."

"My self-esteem is fine." I slipped a black sweater over my head and went to the closet for my good booty-hugging jeans. "I've just learned not to get my hopes up, that's all. Men prefer someone who looks more like you, with the creamy skin and the fake-looking lips and the beauty mark. And your body doesn't look like something some kid made out of play-dough."

"See there?? Why do you say such things about yourself?" Rashida exclaimed, exasperated. "You're always putting down your appearance and it makes no sense. Just because a few men weren't willing to appreciate what you're working with doesn't mean what you have isn't damn good."

I sighed. "Rashida..."

"Your skin is amazing. Your locs are beautiful. You have that sexy, raspy voice. Curvy beyond belief. And I've already told you about your boobs."

"Yes, you've covered that."

"I just named five positive things about you and I could easily name ten more. But I bet you can't. And that's sad, Adele."

I looked over at my friend, who had a glare in her eyes that looked like an uneven mix of pity and frustration. Trudging over and sitting next to her on the bed, I tried to find the right words to make her understand where I was coming from.

"Nate was...one-in-a-million to me," I began, referencing my late husband, admittedly something I didn't do much of. "And he always said I was the same to him. I never believed another man would look at me the way he did, and so far I've been right."

"Adele-"

"No, let me finish," I requested, placing a light hand on her arm. "You're the obvious kind of sexy; men flock to you because of your looks and try to get to know you later. With me, they have to get to know me first *before* they realize there's any kind of attraction, if they ever do. Look at Bradley; he wasn't interested until he realized he liked my sense of humor. And hey; if a man isn't interested, he's just not interested. It is what it is. But please don't think that any lighthearted jabs I take at myself means that I think I'm less than, because I sincerely don't."

Rashida looked at me like she still didn't quite get it. "Then please tell me why you choose to do that; to *take* those jabs at yourself. Why you're *never* willing to believe that someone could fall for everything about you, right off the bat."

I hunched my shoulders. "That's been my reality. It's just easier to put myself in the friend zone than wait for them to do it. You remember when I first started dating again, after Nate passed; I wanted more and they didn't. Yearning for stuff I have no control over doesn't work for me. I might as well just eat a pint of Rocky Road if I'm gonna suffer like that; at least then I get something delicious out of it."

"Girl," Rashida sucked her teeth, giggling as she nudged me with her shoulder. "You'd better not eat anything like that tonight."

"I promise nothing."

"And I guess I can understand what you're saying," she continued. Her smile faded a little. "I still hope you can at least keep an open mind to the possibility of something more than just being a guy's homegirl. You just never know."

"I suppose." I stood, heading over to my vanity. "Whatever happens, happens."

"Okay, can whatever *happens* tonight at least do so while you're in one of those dresses I picked out? Those jeans are cute but there's nothing wrong with kicking things up a notch."

"I'm wearing heels and this clingy shirt; that's enough notch-kicking. And anyway, wearing one of those dresses means I'd have to shave my legs, and I don't have time for all that."

"Fine. At *least* put on some lipstick, though."

"That, I can do."

"Finally, you're listening to me."

"Just trying to get you to hush."

I shooed her out of my room to go hang with Christopher while I finished getting ready. The two of them were camped out on the couch downstairs by the time I was ready to head out, going back and forth about some music video they were watching.

"I'm out," I announced, checking my purse to make sure I had everything. "I won't be back too late."

"You bringing me something back, Ma?" Christopher asked as I grabbed my keys.

"You just ate, boy."

"I'll be hungry again by the time you get home."

"There's other stuff in there you can eat."

"Aww."

"Have fun, girl," Rashida called out, tucking her bare feet underneath her. "Tell Bradley I said hey. And remember what we talked about."

"I got it." I went over and hugged them both, kissing my son on the forehead. "Love y'all."

"Love you, too!" they chorused.

"No dairy, Ma!" Christopher called out as I was closing the front door. I pretended not to hear that.

My mind ran over my conversation with Rashida as I headed to meet Bradley. While I still didn't think this evening was about more than a casual dinner, I tried to convince myself to at least allow the possibility that it *could* be more than that. It wasn't impossible, I supposed.

Who knew, right?

Bradley was waiting for me when I arrived at Houston's. I gave myself a final quick check in the visor mirror before getting out of the car and heading over to him, a smile plastered on my face. I couldn't help but notice how handsome he looked.

"Hey Adele," he greeted me, leaning in for a hug and a kiss on the cheek. "You look great."

"I appreciate that, thanks. So do you."

"Thank you kindly. Ready to eat?"

"Absolutely. I quit eating when you invited me so I'd be good and hungry. Hope you're not expecting me to order salad."

He chuckled as he opened the door to the restaurant, ushering me in ahead of him. He smelled good, too.

After we were seated and placed our orders, Bradley and I fell into some easy conversation. He told me how things were going with his tow truck company, showed me a few pictures of his daughter, chuckled at my stories about Ms. Corine. There were no flirty glances, bites of the bottom lip, or 'accidental' touches of the hand, so I was back to thinking this was just a platonic meet-up. Sure, he was wearing a shirt and tie, but he might've just come from a meeting, for all I knew. We were just sitting around talking and laughing like two old chums. This man wasn't interested in me romantically. If he was, he'd at least do *some* flirting.

"Hey," he said, placing his elbows on the table and leaning towards me slightly. "Would it be inappropriate to tell you how hot you look in that shirt?"

Okay, maybe I was wrong.

"Not at all," I replied, trying to hide my surprise. "I always appreciate a compliment. As long as it's sincere."

"Oh, I'm totally sincere. That top, those jeans...smokin'. *Way* different than when we went out the first time."

Well, damn, I looked that bad on our date? I thought I looked pretty cute that night.

"Well...thanks."

"Did you lose some weight or something?"

Definitely *not* a date.

"Nope. Still as gently overweight as I was when you saw me the last time."

He looked at me in surprise, then busted out laughing.

"Still hilarious!" he chuckled, shaking his head as he took a bite of his steak. "Girl, you are too much."

"Yeah, thanks."

"That's one of the things I like about you, Adele; not a lot of women I've met have that much of a sense of humor. It's refreshing to be around someone who makes me laugh."

"I'm happy to entertain."

"Although," he looked at me as I stuffed some more shrimp into my mouth. "I *do* look forward to finding out more things I like about you. Realizing how funny and cool you are only made me want to get to know you better."

Date-*ish*?

"I look forward to getting to know you better, too. Rashida was always going on and on about what a good guy you are; so far, it seems she was right on the money."

"Rashida is good people. Between you and me, I wanted to ask her out after we met but she was always dating somebody. But it's probably a good thing I didn't try to go there; women *that* fine hardly ever go for me."

So *this* is what being second choice felt like. That's if I was even that; there might have been more women that he was interested in that wasn't as fine as Rashida but finer than me that he couldn't get with, either.

The rest of the evening went like that; him sending these rather mixed signals and me scrambling my brain trying to figure them out. I guess it would have been the sensible thing to just come out and ask but I admittedly didn't know how to phrase the question...

Is this a date-date or a friend-date?

Are you trying to make me your woman? Friends with benefits, perhaps?

Since you like what I'm wearing so much, are you trying to see what's underneath?

I couldn't ask him any of that. And I wasn't usually someone who had trouble just coming out and asking what I wanted to know, but this was different. This time I could be humiliated. That was enough to make me hesitate and question myself, which was even more frustrating than not knowing Bradley's intentions. I was a grown woman; I should be able to ask a simple question.

"You about ready?" Bradley asked once we'd finished dessert. The stupid, non-dairy kind. "Between this good food and sitting over here looking at your hot self all night, I'm ready to get out of here."

"Yeah, sure," I responded, telling myself not to read too much into his statement.

He paid the bill and walked me to my car, his hand placed gently on the small of my back. I had to stop myself from mentally measuring just how far it was from my ass and trying to determine if it was slowly sliding further downward. We just walked as he told me what a great time he had and how glad he was that he asked me out, with a few more compliments sprinkled in. My head was swimming from confusion, and I didn't like the feeling.

This was ridiculous. How was Bradley throwing me off my game so much? I was always preaching how I could tell when a man was interested in me or not, and now look at me; confused as ever. Rashida also constantly said that if a man was into you, you'd know it. But then again, most men were interested in Rashida. So there's that.

"Thanks for meeting up with me, Adele," Bradley said when we reached my car. He smiled as he faced me, his eyes roaming my face. "Wow, you are glowing tonight."

"Yeah? Well, thanks for that. I blame the streetlights."

"No, seriously, Adele...you really are beautiful. Crazy how I didn't realize that until now..."

"You don't have to say that, Bradley."

"I mean it. For real, you really have a lot going for yourself. I admit I only agreed to the blind date at first because I was so cool with Rashida and she was hyping you up so much, but I'm glad I did. It's been a long while since I've had such a good time with a lady."

"Well, I'm glad. I enjoyed this, myself. And I agree; Rashida did good this time. I can sure think of worse things I could've done with my evening than spend it having a delicious meal with a handsome man. A man whose skin is like brown silk, I might add."

He grinned, ducking his head briefly. It had been a while since I made a man blush. Gosh, he was cute.

"Can I see you again?" he asked, stepping closer.

"Of course. I'd like that."

"Good." He was looking at me in a way that I usually would have mistaken as lust, but I could've been wrong. Then he licked his lips. Either they were dry or he wanted to kiss me. "I'm glad to hear that."

We just stood there looking at each other for a few moments. Despite the confusion I was feeling, the desire that was swirling through my body was very clear. I was already attracted to Bradley but that had grown over the course of the evening, and I found myself wanting to taste those lips of his. And the way he was looking at me, it seemed like he wanted the same thing.

So I decided to bite the bullet. When he leaned in, I went for it. Closed my eyes, slightly puckered my lips, and-

"Oh damn...uh, Adele..."

Shit.

"I'm so sorry if I've given you the wrong impression but I...just don't think we should go there." His voice sounded so apologetic. I imagine his expression was probably contrite, as well, but I wouldn't know since I could only bring myself to look at the ground after prying my eyes open. "I like you a lot but I think we should just keep things on the friendship level. I-I hope you understand."

Every inch of my face and body was *flaming* in embarrassment but I managed to force a chuckle and make myself look at his face, taking a (large) step back. "How could I not understand that? You're not feeling me; I get it. That's...that's my bad. Stupid of me to think otherwise."

"No, Adele, don't take it like that-"

"It's fine, Bradley; we don't need to talk about this anymore," I insisted, waving my hands a little too frantically as I took another step back. There was a waver in my voice that I couldn't help. "Just do like I plan to do and erase the last two minutes from your mind. I need to be going..."

"Adele, come on, don't leave like this. Look, I'm sorry; I meant all the stuff I said and I can understand how it would've led you to believe-"

"Totally my fault. I should have known better. Look, um, let's just forget all about this. I'm gonna go 'cause I have some stuff to do at the house and my feet are starting to hurt in these damn heels, anyway." I lunged for my car, fumbling to open the door. "Thanks for dinner or whatever."

"Adele-"

I slammed the door and started the car, screeching out of the parking lot while he was probably still talking. I could only guess because I couldn't make myself look at him again. My hands were literally shaking.

It had been a long time since I felt this stupid. And foolish. Why in the world did I let myself believe that Bradley had *those* kinds of feelings for me? As cute as he was? Men that looked like *that* didn't go for women that looked like *me*. I was no

Rashida, with the creamy sienna skin and tight body. I was just regular. And men didn't want regular. I should've known that by then.

Thankfully, Christopher had dozed off by the time I got home and Rashida had left. She'd sent me a couple of texts asking how the evening went, but there was no way I could admit what happened, at least not yet. I needed the night to process it, shame myself significantly for being so forward and file it away with the other dating fails.

After changing out of my hot-but-meaningless date outfit, I eased downstairs to the kitchen, reached to the back of the freezer, and grabbed my punishment for being such an idiot: raspberry cheesecake gelato.

As if that wouldn't make me feel bad enough, I did something else I had no business doing, especially as upset as I was; I pulled out the photo albums full of pictures of me and Nate.

I let the tears roll as I stuffed my face and looked at pictures of myself getting married to the man I had planned to spend the rest of my life with, but couldn't thanks to an unexpected stroke. The one man who made me feel beautiful, gorgeous, even; who made me feel like the most desired and cherished woman on the planet.

Who had eyes only for me and never let a day go by without telling me how thankful he was for our life together.

The man who gave me a wonderful son. And who had promised to love me and only me until the day he died.

And to his credit, he did.

I missed him *so* much. A woman didn't get a love like the kind I shared with Nate twice in a lifetime. So the sooner I resigned myself to a life of nothing but my son (until he went off to college, at least), work, friends, and platonic dates, the better off I'd be.

At least I had gelato to make me feel better. Until it sent me to the bathroom.

Chapter 4

BLOCKING WHAT HAPPENED with Bradley from my mind would have been a lot easier if he would've stopped calling me.

I made myself talk to him one time and he repeatedly tried to tell me that he didn't mean anything by rejecting me; that he just didn't want to mess up our budding friendship by trying something that might not work out. Sure.

"Adele, I hope you get what I'm trying to say," he pleaded. "I don't want us to stop hanging out or anything. And please don't take what happened the other night personally; it's not that I don't think you're attractive. All that stuff I was saying about how beautiful I think you are, I meant it-"

"I thought we agreed to forget about all that," I reminded him, my voice tired. Having to dredge up that shameful scene sucked whatever energy I had.

"I don't *want* to forget about it. Not until I make sure we're on the same page."

"Sure we are."

"You're just saying that. Come on, Adele, work with me, here. I want us to be good."

"We're fine, Bradley. Yes, the other night was embarrassing but embarrassing stuff happens in life. At least I'm clear on what it is with you now. You don't owe me anything else."

He paused. "I guess I'm just not used to a woman being so...*mature* and calm about this kind of thing. Are you *sure* we're cool?"

"Cool as we can be."

"And we can hang out again?"

"We'll see. Look, Bradley, I have some stuff I need to do so I'll have let you go now. Thanks for calling and trying so hard to soothe my ego; it's nice that you care so much."

"Of course. I *do* care about you, Adele."

"That's sweet, Bradley. I appreciate you saying that. You enjoy the rest of your day, you hear? Kiss that adorable daughter of yours when you see her this weekend. And stay away from those blueberries."

He snickered. "See, that's what I like so much about you," he commented, actually sounding relieved. "You handle stuff like a grown-ass woman instead of getting all in your feelings. I love it. I sure wish more women were like you."

"Oh, I think one of me is plenty. You take care, Bradley."

"Talk to you soon, Adele. Bye."

As soon as I hung up, I blocked his number. Like the grown-ass woman I was.

"SO, WHAT, YOU'RE JUST going to avoid the man forever?"

Rashida looked up at me from the Ninja blender she had picked up. We were in Target so she could spend the gift card she'd won at work, and I was there because I apparently didn't have anything better to do than watch her do that.

"Not *avoid*. More like ignore."

"Adele."

"What? I'm not trying to hold a grudge but I just don't see myself being comfortable enough around him anymore. It's not like we were lifelong buddies or had something deep; we had two dates. Or whatever you want to call them. I'd rather just put him and what happened out of my mind."

"I just hope you don't let this one incident stop you from getting back out there. Just because Bradley didn't have enough sense to see what was right in front of him doesn't mean someone else won't."

"We'll never know."

"Adele!"

"Rashida, don't even bother, okay? I'm not depressed. I'm not distraught. I'm just thinking with a clear head again. What happened with Bradley was humiliating but it was a good reminder to keep my head out of the clouds. I had allowed myself to start wanting something I'd gotten used to not having, *and* had been doing just fine without. Believe me, I'm good."

She put the blender into her red cart and turned to me with a hand on her hip. "So you're just going to spend the rest of your life alone? What if you meet someone who really likes you? Or Bradley has a change of heart and realizes he wants something more than just friendship?"

I figured there was no point in mentioning what Bradley had said about being interested in Rashida but thinking she was out of his league. If he wanted more than friendship with anybody, it was her. But she'd just try to find some way to spin it in my favor, and even though I was mildly curious as to what she could possibly come up with, I didn't even want her to bother.

"There's more to life than having a man," I informed her, playing with the tag on a stovetop griddle. "I have my work, which I love. And these are crucial years for Christopher."

"Crucial how?"

"Before I know it, he'll be going off to college. I need to spend as much time with him now as I can. And I actually love doing that."

"Hmm. And what makes you think your sixteen-year-old, developing, hormone-riddled son is going to want to keep hanging out with you so much? He's already bringing girls to the house. You and I both know there's going to come a time when he's going to prefer hanging with a girlfriend or even his boys over hanging with you."

That might've been true but that didn't mean I loved hearing it. "We'll cross that bridge when we get to it. And anyway, Christopher and I have a special relationship; we've always been close but we got even closer after Nate died. It's been just me and him for years."

"Girl...please don't make the mistake of depending on your son for companionship like that. You need to have a life of your own. What are you going to do when he goes off to college?"

"I'll be by myself. And you'll still be around, or are you planning on moving to the Netherlands?"

"I'll always be here for you, Adele, but there *will* come a day when I'll be settling down with someone, myself. Then a lot of my time will be spent being up under my man. What'll you do then?"

I shrugged. "Guess I'll cross that bridge when I get to it, too."

"Uh-huh. Well, while you're waiting to cross all these bridges, please reconsider this whole being alone thing. You know I loved Nate, but he doesn't have to be the *only* man ever created that will want you and love you. I just refuse to believe that."

"Well, the way things are going-"

"Doesn't mean that's the way things are always going to *be*," Rashida interjected, coming over to stand in front of me. She looked at me with those eyes of hers that I was sure had mesmerized plenty of men. When I first met her, I thought they were contacts. "I'm not saying to settle for just anything. All I'm asking – hoping – is that you're willing to at least keep your heart and mind open to the possibility. You never know *who* God is going to send for you, girl. Or *when*. And I don't want you to brush it off when it happens just because you're afraid of rejection or disappointment."

She looked so sincere. It really did mean a lot to me that she cared about this so much. Even if I didn't exactly share her optimism on my romantic future, I figured it wouldn't hurt to keep an open mind.

Or at least tell her I would.

"I'll try," I told her, adjusting my glasses. "If and when I meet someone else, I'll try to remember to at least give him ample chance before he yanks the rug out from under me and leaves me flat on my face."

Sucking her teeth, Rashida threw up her hands, rolling her eyes like she didn't know what to do with me. "You're impossible."

Rashida would just never understand how it was for me. She couldn't. So I had to do what I thought was best to protect myself from getting my face cracked again, even if it didn't make sense to anyone else.

BETWEEN WORK AND RUNNING Christopher to meetups with his friends and other extracurricular activities, I was pooped. It was Friday night and I got off work a little late, and the thought of cooking dinner actually made me want to cry a little bit. So takeout it was.

I called Christopher to see what he wanted, but he asked if he could go to the movies with his friend Dylan and his dad. Christopher and Dylan had been friends since the fifth grade and I knew Dylan's parents well, so I had no problem with it.

So that meant I could get what I really wanted, and what I wanted was Jamaican food, something Christopher didn't care much for. I called my order in to my favorite spot before heading over, not interested in sitting around waiting. After the week I had, I just wanted to go home, turn some music on and my mind off, and enjoy a quiet Friday evening while I ate some delicious jerk chicken with rice and peas. Maybe even do a couple of my wannabe drawings, too.

Of course, I wasn't the only one satisfying their Jamaican food craving; I could barely find a place to park, the lot was so full. I waited a few extra minutes before going inside the restaurant, hoping that would ensure my food was ready when I got in there.

"It'll be a few more minutes; we're a little backed up," the lady at the counter informed me. Her lovely accent was almost enough to quell my automatic annoyance. "But you can go ahead and pay now, if you like."

Sure they wanted me to go ahead and pay now; I'd be less likely to leave. "That's fine. It'll just be a few more minutes, you say?"

"Yes, just a few minutes. Yours should be next up."

"All right, thank you."

I paid my bill, then eased over to the side so the person behind me could be told their order wasn't ready, either. I glanced at my phone, checking whatever email or app notifications that had come in during my drive there. Might as well get in a few games of Bejeweled.

"Damn."

I glanced up, figuring someone was on the phone or had gotten the wrong food order or something, but to my surprise there was a man looking right at me. After peeking over my shoulder to see what else he could have been leering at in such a way, I turned back to him, eyebrows raised. "Damn what?"

"Damn, you're *fire*. You've had my attention since you walked in here."

Momentarily stumped, I had to mentally alert myself that my mouth was hanging open. Clamping it shut, I cleared my throat and gave him a gracious nod. "Well...thanks. Unless there's some unpleasant reason for that."

"Not at all. And to think I almost went somewhere else for my dinner tonight. Thank god the place down the street failed their health inspection."

"I think the bullet you dodged on that trumps whatever fleeting pleasure you think you have from meeting me."

"I hope it's not just fleeting. And we haven't officially met yet." He stepped closer to me, and I got a better view of this man with good looks that were almost intimidating. I'd never been a huge fan of goatees but on him, yes. *Lawd* yes. "I'm Kingston. Kingston Farrell."

He was holding his hand out to me. I glanced at it before returning the gesture, shaking his hand gently before easing away. This was ridiculous; he could be a hand model. "Adele."

"Nice to meet you, Adele."

I prayed that my order would come up right that second, but no such luck. The orders the woman at the counter was placing in bags were going to other people, not me. I glanced at the number on my receipt; number 49. Mine *had* to be next. I didn't want to keep standing there with this beautiful man who was clearly just trying to keep himself occupied while he waited for his oxtail.

"Yeah, nice meeting you, too," I felt obliged to say. This was where I'd normally tack on questions about if he'd eaten there before or if he was from around here, but figured there was no point. There was no need in small talk with someone I was never going to see again.

"I'd love to sit somewhere with you and eat together, whenever we both get our food," Kingston continued. "This isn't the best environment to get to know a lady I'm interested in."

Lil' boy, go on somewhere. Of course I had no idea how old this man was, but I was sure he was younger than me. And I didn't know what kind of game he was playing but I wasn't in the mood for it.

"Did somebody point me out to you and bet that you wouldn't be able to get my number or something?"

"What?"

"You're messing with me. You have to be."

He had the nerve to try to look confused. "Why would you say that?"

"Because I can't imagine why you would be trying this - whatever you're doing - so hard unless you had something to gain from it."

"I *hope* to gain your interest and your number so I can get to know you. Not sure why that's so unbelievable."

"Oh, I get it," I realized, shifting my weight and placing a hand on my hip. "Rashida put you up to this, didn't she?"

"Who?"

"Don't do that. You're cute but the game isn't. Rashida knows I like to get takeout from here on Friday nights, so she somehow got you to come and carry out this pity mission. Which picture did she use, so you'd know what I looked like? I hope it was a decent one, at least."

He held up his hands. "I swear I have no idea what you're talking about, Adele. I'm not trying to play with you; that's some bullshit I barely did in college, let alone now. I came over to you because I wanted to; because I see an attractive woman that sparked my interest enough to put myself out there and approach. That's it."

I'll admit, he was good at this because he definitely sounded sincere. I wondered how often he did this kind of thing. Or maybe he was just a natural.

"Okay, I'll take your word for it," I replied, trying to keep the sarcasm out of my voice. "Still, though, I'm sure a young man as handsome as yourself can find someone a little more suited for you. I'm just a regular widow with a teenaged son."

"Oh, wow. You're a widow?"

"Yeah. Sexy, huh? So I'll do you a favor and let you off the hook so you can go find some pretty young thing to paint the town red with tonight."

"I already met the pretty young thing I want to get to know." He was giving me a look that might have moistened me up if I didn't know any better. But thankfully I did. "So...how 'bout I just give you *my* number, and when or if you decide to check my sincerity, you can give me a call."

"Number 49!"

Finally. I breathed a small sigh of relief as I excused myself and moved around the growing number of people to get my food. When I turned around to head for the door, Kingston stood in my path, holding out his card, eyes on me.

"Please take it," he requested. "I really want to hear from you."

He was a nice guy. Or doing a damn good job of acting like one. So there was no need to be rude to the youngin'. I'd take his number, but that didn't mean I had to use it.

I wordlessly took his card and slid it into my pocket, giving him a tight smile. His return smile looked pleased and a little relieved.

"Don't just toss that in the gutter once you get outside," he playfully ordered, still showing those white teeth. Geesh, he was pretty. "I can't prove myself to you if you don't give me a chance to."

"I'll keep that in mind," I droned good-naturedly. And anyway, I had no intention of throwing his card in the gutter.

That would be rude. I'd at least wait until I got home and put it in the regular trash.

Sidestepping him, I got a whiff of his cologne and momentarily closed my eyes in appreciation before I could stop myself. Yummy-smelling men had always been something of a weakness.

"You have a good evening, Kingston," I told him, giving an over-the-shoulder glance as I grabbed the door handle.

"You too, Adele."

I was back in my car before I realized my heart was beating a little faster than usual. Okay, so I was attracted to him. He was damn handsome. *Too* handsome; Kingston's looks lapped Bradley's by three. Which was why I was even more convinced that Rashida had something to do with this supposedly-chance meeting.

As soon as I was back home, I called her. And I wasted no time getting to the point.

"Where do you get off trying to set me up when I explicitly told you I wasn't trying to go there with anybody?"

"Excuse me? What are you talking about?"

"I'm talking about the man you sent to stake out my favorite Jamaican spot and try to run some game on me. I'll admit, you picked a good one; buddy was hot. But I still don't appreciate it. Especially since we *just* talked about this the other day!"

"Adele, do you really think I would blatantly go against your wishes like that? And anyway, you know me; if I wanted to set you up with somebody, I'd just tell you. I don't need to play games with it."

She had a point, I admit. She had set me up with Bradley and there was no trickery involved; just a lot of arm-twisting to get me to agree.

"I'm a little hurt that you think I'd do that, girl," Rashida continued. "Of course I remember everything you said the other day. Whether or not I agree with you brushing all men off indefinitely, that's *your* decision to make. We've been friends for damn near twenty years. I would *never* go behind your back, especially when you feel as strongly about something as you do this. Damn, you don't know that by now?"

Now I felt ridiculous. "Rashida, girl...you're right. I'm so sorry. I just got it in my head that there had to be some unnatural reason that Kingston approached me, and I concocted some foolishness and ran with it. Please forgive me for that."

She sucked her teeth.

I paused. "Does that mean you *do* or-"

"Hush. You know I forgive you."

"Thank you."

"Though I don't know why it's so hard to believe that the man could sincerely be interested in you."

"You didn't see him. He's the kind of good-looking that snatches your breath; warms you up just by looking at you. Scrambles your brain. Makes you wanna risk stuff. I feel kind of silly even saying all that, but it's the truth."

"I don't have to see him to think that's ridiculous. It doesn't matter *how* handsome he is, that doesn't make it unfathomable that he could have a genuine interest in *you*. Whether you want to date anyone right now or not, I wish you would stop underestimating yourself."

"I'm not doing that. I'm just not trying to make a fool out of myself again."

"Adele, sweetie, what happened with Bradley happened with *Bradley*. That's *one* man. Please don't go thinking that all men are going to see you as he saw you. At least give this Kingston a fair shot before you write him off. Unless you're just not attracted to him."

Oh, I couldn't say that at all. I was still a functioning woman. I'd be imagining that black wavy tapered cut, thick dark eyebrows and goatee, juicy-looking lips, and what seemed like a *very* nice hard body underneath the mock turtleneck and slacks he was wearing quite a few times. Probably later on that night. While I played with my bedside toys.

But that didn't mean I needed to take it any further than that. Fantasies were harmless.

"Fine, yes, I'm attracted to him," I admitted. "But I'd just rather let him stay in my memory as the hot young man I met one Friday night and leave it at that. I don't have the energy for another dead end."

A few quiet moments passed. "All right, girl," Rashida finally conceded, her voice soothing my inexplicable nerves. "Whatever you want to do. You know I've got your back either way."

Chapter 5

"SO WHAT'S *this* one's name?"

"Zuri. She's real cool, Ma. And she doesn't want to be all up on me all the time like Deena did."

"Well, congratulations."

"You're being sarcastic, aren't you?"

"Maybe."

"How can you not like her already?"

"I never said I didn't like her, baby," I replied, going over to the fridge to get some salad dressing. "It's just that every other week you come home swooning over some new girl like the last one didn't even exist. I never thought I'd be raising a little Cassanova."

"I don't know what that means. But if that's some old way of saying I'm a player, I'm not."

I paused in opening the salad dressing bottle and quirked a brow. "Old?"

"You know what I mean. Old-*fashioned.*"

"Uh-huh."

Christopher ran a hand over the reddish-brown hair that he inherited from Nate. He needed a haircut. "I'm not a player. Sometimes I just like a girl at first then realize I don't anymore after I spend some time with her. But I'm always honest with them, just like you always tell me to be. And I try to be nice about it."

"Well, that's good at least. I'm glad to hear that part."

"You know what else is good about Zuri?"

"What?"

"Her dad is single. And when I showed her a picture of you, she said that we should hook y'all up."

"Oh, no thank you," I quickly retorted, holding up a hand. "Not interested."

"How come? You don't have a boyfriend, do you?"

Hesitating slightly, I concentrated on the bell pepper I'd just started slicing. "No..."

"I can show you his picture. He's not ugly."

"Doesn't matter what he looks like, Christopher. I'm just not interested."

I could feel Christopher eyeing me as I continued chopping the vegetables. I couldn't imagine what must have been going through his mind. What I didn't want was for him to press me on why I didn't want to meet his girlfriend's dad. That was a hard enough conversation to have with Rashida; I certainly didn't want to try to explain it to my sixteen-year-old son.

Of course, I could always just say it was grown folks' business.

A few more quiet moments passed with Christopher absently pushing his phone around on the island and me preparing a salad. I knew he was going to say something else about all this; I could only wonder what.

"Ma, are you gay?"

I dropped my knife. I definitely wasn't expecting *that*.

I glanced down at the knife on the floor but left it there. Putting a hand on my hip, I frowned at my inquisitive son. "Excuse me?"

"Are you? I don't care either way but I can't help but be curious."

"*Why* would you be curious??"

"Because your dates with men never seem to work out; you only go out with them once or twice before it's over. And I heard you say something to Auntie Rashida the other day about not wanting to bother with any more men. Then I suggest introducing you to Zuri's dad and you automatically say no. I just wonder if you don't like men anymore, that's all."

"Wow," I muttered, slowly stooping to get the fallen knife. Moving over to place it in the sink, I tucked some locs behind my ear and adjusted my glasses. "Christopher, I am not gay. Not even close."

He eyed me. "You sure?"

"Am I...yes, I'm *sure*!"

"If you say so. I just don't get why you would want to stay by yourself. Dad died years ago. Is it because you miss him so much or something?"

"Of course I miss your father, baby," I confirmed, grabbing another knife and resuming my vegetable mutilation. "I miss him every day. But that's got nothing to do with why I don't want to meet Zuri's dad or anyone else."

"Ma, if you're having trouble keeping a man, why don't you do something to...I don't know...fix yourself up a little bit? Wear something other than jeans, put on a little makeup..."

"I wear makeup, Christopher."

"Well, something else, then. Whatever you need to do."

My hand slowed as I looked up at him in realization. "Baby...do I embarrass you?"

"No, Ma." He quickly stood from the stool in front of the island, grabbing his phone. "I wasn't trying to say that. Um, do I have time to go back upstairs before you're done fixing dinner?"

Pursing my lips as I felt a rush of something cold hit me and send goosebumps sprouting up my bare arms, I just nodded. I turned to the back counter as he left the room, looking down at the dish towel I had tossed there until my glasses fogged up.

I STILL HADN'T THROWN Kingston's card away. The bigger part of me said I would, but the tiny, flattered part of me wanted to hang onto it, even if I didn't use it.

I was admittedly curious to hear what he would say if I actually called. Mostly, though, I wondered if he'd even remember me. How many other women did he hit on that night? Or *since* then? It had been a few days; who knew how many cards he'd given out in that time. I could've been one of many.

Thinking like this fueled my justification to not call him. I might've been a teeny bit intrigued, just based off of attraction alone. But all I had to do was remember poking my lips out to Bradley and him shutting me down and I was reminded why I didn't want to go there again. He had just been the latest in a string of men in the past few years to like me, but not like me like *that*. It never failed; I was cool as hell, fun to be with, great for a laugh, but that's where it stopped. There was almost never any attraction on a romantic level.

As much as I loved being a good friend – and I really did - it would've been nice to be looked at as more than that. But it wasn't looking like it was in the cards for me. I'd had it once, and lost it when Nate died. I'd had my turn.

I'd never admit it out loud, not even to Rashida; but I just couldn't tolerate trying to find love anymore.

I ALLOWED MYSELF ONE night to muse and wallow in all of this stuff before I made myself push it out of my mind. A pity party wasn't going to change anything. And I had plenty of other great stuff in my life to focus on and be thankful for.

After dropping Christopher off at basketball practice the next day, I headed over to see Dad. I made sure to call first, just to make sure he was there; he was technically retired but he still did handyman work when he wanted to. There was only so much sitting around the house Dad was gonna do.

"Come on in!" he yelled when I rang the doorbell.

I eased the door open, the jazz sounds getting louder as I headed to the back of the house. Dad was sitting out on the sun porch, drinking and putting together a puzzle.

"Hey there," he greeted, glancing up at me with that half-smile.

"Hey, Dad." I leaned down to give him a hug before taking a seat in the wicker chair near him. "Brought you some meat loaf and greens."

"I appreciate it. Now I won't have to mess with that other stuff in there."

"What other stuff? Oh yeah, I forgot your admirers keep you fed nowadays."

"I keep tellin' these ladies that I don't need them to bring me anything else, but they don't listen. I guess they think keeping my belly full will sweep me off my feet or somethin'."

"Wow, Dad," I giggled, shaking my head. "Sure wish I had it like you."

"No ya don't. 'Cause I want to be left alone and you want to find somebody."

My smile faded slightly as I looked at him in surprise. "What makes you think that?"

"You date, don't ya?"

"I mean, yeah...but that doesn't necessarily mean I want to *find* somebody."

"So what's the point of doing it?"

"Hmph," I grunted, sliding my chair a little closer so I could peruse the puzzle pieces with him. "That's the very question I've been asking myself, lately."

Dad looked over at me as if he expected me to elaborate, but I just pretended to be engrossed in piecing together the scattered cornfield image in front of us. When he saw I was going to leave it at that, he took a sip of his whiskey.

"How's my grandson?" he asked after a few quiet moments.

"Doing really good. Gonna have to get him from practice in a while."

"Season going all right?"

"Only lost one game so far. They've got a great team this year."

"Let me know when the next one is and I'll try to get over there."

"Sure will; he'll love that." I mindlessly pushed around some puzzle pieces with my fingertips. "There *is* one thing that kind of concerns me about Christopher, though."

"What's that?" Dad asked, looking over at me.

"I get that he's a walking ball of hormones and all that, but I wasn't quite expecting *this* level of girl-crazy," I admitted. "Ever since he grew a few inches and got that baby mustache, he's coming home talking about a different girl every week, seems like."

"Sounds about par to me. Boys that age are like kids in a candy store."

"Yeah, but still. I just worry that all this attention is going to tempt him to do something he's not ready to do. Or that *I'm* not ready for him to do. I've already had bad dreams about him coming home telling me he's knocked somebody up."

"You done caught a girl in his room or something? Caught him in a lie or sneakin' around?"

"No, nothing like that. Guess I'm just pre-worrying."

"Nothing wrong with keepin' your eyes open. But don't be over there stressin' yourself over something that hasn't even happened yet. He's a good boy who knows right from wrong but that don't mean he won't make mistakes. You've gotta let him learn from 'em."

"Yeah. True enough, I can't watch him every second. Though part of me still wishes I could."

"You can't keep babying that boy. He's damn near seventeen."

"I know, I know." I paused, wondering if I wanted to say what else was on my mind. "There's something else."

"What?"

"I think...I think I embarrass Christopher." My cheeks flamed a little bit, not thrilled that this was even an issue.

"What makes you think that?"

"He apparently thinks I can't keep a man. Suggested I 'fix myself up.' Actually asked if I was gay when I shut down his suggestion to fix me up with his new girlfriend's dad. Can't say I loved hearing that."

"Hmm." Dad pressed a piece into the corner section, then smoothed a finger over it. "Are ya?"

"No!"

"So you go out on these dates and then change your mind? Why even bother if you're not interested?"

I adjusted my glasses, hating that I had even started this conversation. My voice was low when I admitted, "It's not usually *me* that loses interest, Dad."

Dad looked over at me.

"In case you haven't noticed – and I know you have – I'm not exactly glamorous," I continued. "There's nothing about me that wows men like that, at least physically. As far as personality goes, they love me. But that's where it stops."

"Feeling sorry for yourself?"

"Not at all. Just stating facts."

"God made you like He made you for a reason," Dad told me, pressing in another puzzle piece. "Hope you're not being foolish and thinkin' there's something wrong with how ya are just 'cause a few men don't appreciate what they see."

"I'm not doing that. At least, I'm not trying to. I've always been fine with how I am. My hair, glasses, broad nose, thick thighs; don't have a problem with any of it. But I'm... not what men go for. That's just been my experience; it is what it is. Guess I didn't realize it was so glaring until recently."

"You just ain't met the right one yet, that's all," Dad concluded with a wave of his hand. "And I bet he'll show up when you ain't even expectin' him to."

"If you say so."

"You just can't be stubborn when he does, actin' like you don't want nobody."

Even though I had said that myself several times recently, I still asked, "Who said I didn't?"

"I bet you're *actin'* like you don't, regardless of what you're sittin' here sayin' in front of me. Don't act like I don't know how you do. It was just like when you were in high school and that group of girls kept leaving you out of stuff. They weren't mean to you, but didn't include you like you wished they would. So you acted like you didn't care one way or the other."

Damn, I had forgotten about that. "I guess I can see the correlation but this isn't quite the same thing."

"It don't have to be the exact same thing. Same concept. Just don't go lying to yourself, is all I'm sayin'. Ain't nothin' wrong with wanting somebody to spend your life with. Or being disappointed that you ain't found it yet."

That conversation stayed on my mind after I left Dad's an hour or so later. I had told Rashida I'd go out with her that night, even though I wasn't feeling it. After I picked up Christopher, fixed dinner and took a shower, everything in me just wanted to fall across my bed and stay there until morning. But Rashida had hounded me into submission and I knew she'd raise hell if I tried to back out.

So I got all cleaned and oiled and prettied up and met Rashida out at our favorite spot, Barfly. As usual, she had the cleavage on display and her trademark purple lipstick. It was still funny to me how much energy she had put into trying to find just the right shade.

"Hey, girl," she greeted me as I approached the sidewalk where she stood. "I was just about to call you."

"There was some accident that held up the traffic but I'm here now," I droned, leaning in for a hug. "How long are we gonna be here?"

She glanced at her watch before quirking a brow at me. "Twenty seconds to complaining. A new record."

"I came, didn't I? I'd much rather be at home watching a movie with Christopher or something."

"I keep telling you, you can't depend on that boy for your entertainment forever. Might as well start weaning yourself off of him now. And it'll do you good to get out of that house and enjoy yourself. You're looking great; god, I wish I had your hips. I love that dress on you."

"Thanks. As do you, but I guess I don't have to tell you that, with all the attention you're getting just standing here."

She waved me off without even bothering to look around and see what I was talking about. Several men were checking her out, but she was oblivious. That was one thing I could admit about Rashida; she might have attracted a lot of attention but it wasn't because she actively sought it out. She just went about her business. That was more than I could say about a lot of women with her kind of beauty.

Once we were inside, I tried not to look at my watch every two minutes. I enjoyed a night out every now and then, but that particular night, I just wasn't into it. As usual, most male eyes were on Rashida as we made our way over to the bar, while hardly anyone paid me any attention. Playing the sidekick to my beautiful homegirl wasn't something I was in the mood for.

Sighing, I ordered a rum and Coke and told myself to try to have a good time while I was there. I needed to put all this foolishness about not being wanted out of my mind; before that whole scene with Bradley, it wasn't something I thought about much at all. But since then, it had been stuck in my head and I hated it. I thought I'd gotten past all that insecure crap in college.

"Quite the crowd in here tonight," Rashida commented, looking around as she sipped her champagne. "Guess a lot of people needed to take their minds off things for a while."

"I suppose. Though I never considered that to be a reason why people partied."

"Well, I can't speak for anybody else but I know it's a reason for me. Working in Human Resources can be a pain in the ass and coming out to dance and drink and hear some good music just melts my stress away and lets me forget about all the nonsense."

"You can't dance and drink and listen to music at home?"

"Not the same and you know it."

"I guess. Isn't that one of the owners right there?" I asked, pointing to a walking hunk of dark chocolate that was talking to a couple of people nearby. Plenty of the ladies in there were checking him out.

"Oh yeah, Roland Bell," Rashida confirmed, eying him as she tapped her glass to her lips for a moment, then apparently caught herself, turning around on her barstool. "Let me stop;

I don't need to be lusting after a married man. And he is notoriously committed to his wife so these women making eyes at him are wasting their time."

"You mean like you were just doing?"

"Shut up. I can appreciate the view but you know I don't mess with married men."

"Yeah, I know." I sipped my drink, feeling myself relax a tiny bit. My shoulders began moving to the music a little. "I have to admit, it *is* nice to be out among the grown folks with some libations and son of a *bitch*!"

Rashida's head whipped around in alarm. "What? What's wrong??"

I couldn't believe my eyes. I actually lifted my glasses, then remembered that I was near-sighted.

"Adele, what's the matter?" Rashida pressed, grabbing my arm and looking in the direction I was marveling at.

Swiveling around on my barstool, I tried to gather myself and hope he didn't see me.

"It's Kingston."

Chapter 6

"WELL, MY NIGHT JUST got better."

So he spotted me. I didn't think I was all that distinctive but Kingston had somehow scoped me between all the mingling bodies and was now standing right behind me at the bar. I could smell his cologne without even seeing him.

"How are you, Adele?"

Rashida gave me a little kick to the ankle, encouraging me to turn around and acknowledge Kingston. There was no telling what was going through her mind right then.

Clearing my throat, I silently told myself to quit acting like I'd never met a man before and get it together.

Swiveling back around, I slid a smile onto my face and tried not to notice that he somehow looked even better than he did when we met.

"Hello, Kingston," I replied smoothly. "I'm great, thanks. How 'bout yourself?"

"Same. Especially now that we've run into each other. I was getting the feeling you weren't going to call me."

"Don't take it personally. I just have a lot going on."

"I get it. But I'm definitely glad to see you now, though."

His eyes hadn't left me at all during this exchange, and I could feel Rashida sitting there looking back and forth between us.

"I'm sorry; I'm being rude," I caught myself, glancing at my smirking friend. "Kingston, this is Rashida; best friend a lady can have. Rashida, girl, this is Kingston; fellow lover of Jamaican cuisine."

"Hey, Kingston; nice to meet you," Rashida greeted him, grinning way too hard.

"Same here," Kingston replied, graciously nodding at her before turning his eyes back to me. "Hopefully you can become my ally and get your girl here to give me a chance."

"I don't know; she can be pretty stubborn..."

My jaw dropped. "Thanks a lot..."

"I can handle stubborn," Kingston insisted, still eyeing me in a way that woke my skin up. Tingles were spreading like an exhilarating rash and I both loved and hated the feeling. "Unless she just flat-out asks me to step off, I don't give up that easily."

I didn't have to look at Rashida to know she was loving this. She liked this man, which meant she was going to be on my back nonstop to let my guard down. Especially since I had already admitted to being attracted to him. I was already kicking myself for that.

"I like that," Rashida commented, confirming my thoughts. I glared at her but she just smiled wider and winked at me. "And I *hope* she doesn't do something as silly as telling you to step off prematurely. You two should get to know each other better."

"Couldn't agree more," Kingston concurred. "But I'm more than willing to move at her pace. As long as I get to stay in the picture, I can be as patient as I need to be."

"We'll see if you're still saying the same thing in six months," Rashida chuckled. "'Cause, *dude*-"

"Um, excuse me?" I interjected. "Can y'all stop talking like I'm not sitting right here?"

"Well hell, *you* aren't saying anything," Rashida retorted. Grabbing her drink, she slid off the barstool. "Here, Kingston, take my seat. That way you two can heap *all* of your attention on each other."

"Ahh, I don't think that's necessary," I quickly protested, trying to shoot Rashida a *what-are-you-doing* glare that she pretended not to notice. "I'm sure Kingston would rather hang with his friends or whoever he came with than sit over here with me."

"On the contrary," Kingston wasted no time replying, moving closer to Rashida's vacated seat. "I came with my cousin but we don't need to babysit each other. Besides, he knows what the deal is; if I meet someone, he's on his own. He does the same to me."

"Oh." I couldn't decide what my disappointment-to-relief ratio was over this. The fact that I was relieved at all was enough to throw me for a loop. I was just supposed to want him to go on about his business and that's it.

"But if you'd rather I left you alone, I'll respect that," Kingston continued, looking right at me. His voice was serious. "I'm not trying to make you uncomfortable."

Damn him for looking so genuine. He really seemed like he meant that.

"It's fine," I heard myself say. "You can sit down here, if you want."

Kingston's broad smile returned as he eased himself onto the barstool.

"Have fun!" Rashida exclaimed over her shoulder as she shimmied away, immediately being approached by a broad-shouldered gentleman. It never failed.

I could feel Kingston looking at me and the pressure to make some kind of witty repartee was causing my throat to close up. Usually, I wasn't that uncomfortable around men. That was part of the reason they always thought I was so cool to hang with (and to have as a *friend*). But I wasn't feeling as at ease with Kingston as I usually felt with guys. He didn't make me uncomfortable in a bad way, though, which was totally the problem. And it was throwing me off.

"You probably think I'm full of shit, huh?"

Glancing at him in slight alarm, I adjusted the neckline of my dress. "That's an interesting first question."

"I figure it's either that, or you think I'm some kind of player. Or you're just sincerely not attracted to me."

That wasn't it. That damn sure wasn't it. But I certainly wasn't about to tell him that.

"I don't know you," is what I said. "And I'm a little surprised that someone like you would be at all interested in someone like me."

He frowned curiously. "What do you mean by that? Someone like what?"

A man who is way too fine to be trying to hit on somebody whose thigh firmness went out with the Wop. "I'm guessing you're younger than me. How old *are* you, if you don't mind my asking?"

"I'm thirty-three."

Ehh. Not as bad as I thought. "I see."

"You want another drink?"

"Uhh, yeah, sure." I eyed him as he asked the bartender for another rum and Coke for me and some Hennessey for himself. Once we were both sipping on our drinks, I couldn't help but press, "You're not gonna ask how old *I* am now?"

He shook his head. "Nah. For one, I know that's like a cardinal sin for a lot of ladies. But more importantly, I don't care. You're grown so that's really all I need to know, as far as that."

"That I am," I replied, unable to resist the small smile creeping onto my face.

"I'm sure that'll be one of the many pieces of information that I'll learn about you as we continue getting to know each other, anyway," Kingston continued. "If you allow that."

"Are you going to try to convince me to do that by saying that us running into each other again was some kind of serendipitous cosmic hook-up?"

Chuckling, he set his glass down on the bar. "Nah, I wouldn't say all that. I recently moved to the area so if you live here, I don't suppose it's all that improbable that we'd see each other around town. What I *will* say, though, is that I believe everything happens for a reason. And there has to be a reason I was so drawn to you from the moment I saw you get out of your car the other night at the restaurant. Or why I haven't been able to get you out of my mind since. Or why I stopped thinking about anything else when I saw you sitting over here tonight."

Oh, he was *good*.

"You sure it's not just the big ass?" I joked, trying to quell the growing interest that I didn't want to have.

"Not gonna act like I haven't noticed that..." he admitted with a bite of the lip, then arched one of those shiny dark brows. "...Or that I don't think it's hot..."

Don't you dare get aroused, Adele...

"But there are women with big asses all over the place," he continued. "That's not the only thing that catches my eye. I'm trying to get closer to everything about you, Adele, not just your body."

Part of me wanted to get up, go find Rashida, and leave this young(er) man sitting there with his smooth talk and Hennessey. But I stayed right there, falling into a frustratingly easy rapport with Kingston. And if I'm honest, the longer we sat at that bar, the more he steadily chipped away at the wall I had hastily thrown up after the Bradley incident. Maybe it hadn't been long enough for my resistance to be strong enough yet, or Kingston was a master charmer. Whatever it was, I was sincerely enjoying his company.

He even cajoled me onto the dance floor for some semi-slow swaying, which had *definitely* not been in the plans. But I let him put his hands on my waist and pull me closer to him. I let him rest his cheek against mine. I let him whisper stuff in my ear about what a good time he was having with me.

And I let myself enjoy all of it.

Despite that, though, I still believed that whatever spell I had inadvertently cast over Kingston would dissipate soon enough. Maybe he had just gone through a bad breakup and his discernment was off; I could be the total opposite of whoever it was he left, or whoever left him. He just wanted to try another flavor for a minute before going back to his usual cuisine. This was all temporary.

I might have told myself all of this but I didn't quite buy it. Even though I clearly wasn't an expert in gauging men's physical attraction towards me, I could usually tell when they're just straight full of shit. And I honestly never got that vibe from Kingston.

It just would have been *so* much easier for me if I had.

After another couple of hours, both my feet and my watch were indicating it was time to go. My days of hanging out all night were long gone, and I did have to work the next morning. Rashida was already hanging out near the door and giving occasional glances in our direction, clearly not wanting to interrupt us. Not that I would have totally minded if she had.

Kingston insisted on walking us to our cars, and we went to Rashida's first. As he wished her good night, I watched closely for any spark or sign of muted interest on his part; any last-ditch flirtations, excuses for touching, double entendres. But there was none of that. He was polite, but platonic. He didn't touch her; just closed her door once she was safely tucked into her driver's seat and gave a slight nod. She signaled for me to call her before driving off, leaving me and Kingston standing there alone.

"Where's your car?" he asked me.

"It's over there," I pointed a little ways down the lot, already turning in that direction. "You can just stand here and watch until I get over there; you don't have to actually walk-"

"Not an option," he interjected, gently taking my elbow as we headed for my car. "Come on, now."

Neither of us said much of anything as we strolled across the parking lot, his hands in his pockets and mine gripping my purse. I mindlessly watched it bounce repeatedly against my thighs, still not totally believing that this incredibly smooth, charming, handsome man who smelled like orgasmic deliciousness had stuck to my side the whole evening.

"I'm so glad I saw you tonight," he told me once we reached my Nissan. "You made my evening."

Grinning (because I couldn't help it), I ducked my head and adjusted my glasses. "That's flattering, Kingston. Can't deny I enjoyed myself with you, too."

"Good. Because I can tell you still have a guard up. But like I said earlier, I can be patient for what I want." He stepped closer. "And I'm more than willing to prove myself to you, Adele."

His words, the look in his eyes, his cologne, and just *him* were all mixing into a concoction more potent that those rum and Cokes I had earlier. My breathing deepened a little as I rested my eyes on his, admiring the deep amber brown in the streetlight. Once I committed those to memory, my gaze slid down past his proportional broad nose to his lips that looked as soft as marshmallows. And likely just as tasty.

"I'd love to call you," he was saying, meeting my gaze again after finishing his own silent perusal of me that I'd been too busy ogling to notice. "But if you're not feeling that yet, can I at least get you to promise to consider using that card I gave you?"

Not trusting myself to speak just yet, I just opened my purse and pulled out one of my own cards. I had them for work but hardly ever gave them out; it wasn't like I did a lot of networking. Forgot I had the damn things most of the time.

"You sure?" Kingston asked, glancing at the card before looking back at me intently. "Please don't feel pressured."

"No pressure here," I assured him. "I don't do pity offerings of my phone number. You wouldn't be getting this if I didn't want you to have it."

"That's all I need to know, then," he replied, quickly plucking it from between my fingers and giving it a quick scan before sliding it into his pants pocket. "And you damn sure don't have to worry about me taking this just to be taking it. You *will* be hearing from me, Adele. Soon."

"Oh, I believe you." I really did. I felt my smile widening all on its own and I caught myself, ducking my head slightly again. Goodness, I hadn't been this bashful since I was crushing on my Biology lab partner in college. I unlocked my car door and silently told myself, again, to get it together.

He leaned forward and planted a gentle kiss to my forehead. "Be safe getting home, Adele," he instructed in a low voice, stepping aside as he opened my car door for me. I could feel his eyes as I lowered myself into the car, praying I didn't bump my head or do something equally as dorky. But I managed.

"Talk to you soon, Kingston," I said, starting the car.

"Yes, you will." He winked at me before closing the door and taking a few steps back. I didn't even realize my whole body was vibrating as I pulled out of the parking lot, with him watching me.

I had managed to calm and gather myself by the time I got home and took another hot shower. Rashida had already sent me a string of texts, asking how things went and telling me she'd pull my hair if I hadn't given Kingston my number. Before I could respond to her foolishness, though, Kingston called.

"Double-checking to make sure the number I gave you was real?" I quipped when I answered the phone. I knew it was him, even though his number wasn't saved in my phone yet. Guess I spent so much time mulling over the card he gave me when we met that it had stuck in my memory.

"Well, I figured since your card had both your office and cell number on there, my chance was pretty good," Kingston replied, amusement in his voice. "And anyway, you seem too mature to be giving out fake numbers."

"You've got me, there."

"I just wanted to talk to you for a minute before I took it in for the night. You good? How's your son doing?"

Christopher wasn't a subject we had gotten too deep into during the evening but I thought it was cool of him to ask. "Oh, he was good and knocked out by the time I got home. Phone glued to his hand, as usual."

Kingston chuckled. "Sounds about right. How old is he, again?"

"Sixteen."

"Hopefully we can get to the point where I tell you about some of the stuff I did when I was sixteen. It's pretty entertaining stuff."

"I can just imagine," I replied with a smile as I sat on my bed and started spreading lotion over my legs.

"You never mentioned how *you* were doing."

"You just saw me about an hour ago, Kingston."

"Things can change in sixty minutes. You might've been feeling me when we parted ways but had second thoughts since then. Please tell me that's not the case."

I paused my leg-lotioning. "That's...not the case."

"Good." He actually sounded relieved, which made my smile stretch. "Well, look, I know it's late and we both have to work tomorrow; I won't keep you. I just wanted to call to say good night. And hear that voice again."

"There's nothing special about my voice."

"I completely disagree. You've got that sexy, raspy thing going on that I love. I wouldn't be surprised if you could sing, too."

"Couldn't carry a tune if you put handles on it."

"Really? That's wild. But whatever. I'm good with just hearing you talk."

I couldn't help blushing. Rashida was the only one who had ever really commented on my voice; I always thought it was too deep and actually used to hate it back in the day. Kingston was the first man to rave about it.

"I'm not sure what to do with all this flattery, Kingston," I finally said, closing the lotion bottle and setting it on the nightstand. "If you're trying to butter me up or something, you don't have to use so much butter."

"You'll learn this the closer we get; I don't say anything I don't mean," Kingston's informed, his voice strong and clear. "That, and I give credit where it's due. So you might as well just get used to all this 'cause once you become my woman, this will be a regular thing."

I paused in removing my glasses. Did he really just say that?

"Not trying to freak you out," he continued when I hadn't responded after a few moments. I could actually *hear* his smile. "Just letting you know."

Clearing my throat, I ran a hand through my locs. "Umm..."

"Get some rest, Adele. I'll call you tomorrow." He gently hung up, leaving me still sitting there gaping about that *once you become my woman* prediction.

He sounded so sure about it, too. It wasn't a question at all.

And...it was a little hot, I had to admit.

But I made myself dismiss it. Even though he insisted he only said things that he meant, I told myself that it was a shock value comment. He liked to keep me on my toes. I'd have to keep my eyes all the way open with Kingston; I could tell already.

True to his word, Kingston called me the next day. I was heading out to lunch and he wasted no time letting me know what he wanted.

"Can I take you out?"

I paused. "Like...on a date?"

"Of course."

"A *romantic* date?"

"What other kind is there?"

"Figured you might just want to...hang out. Keep it platonic."

"If that's what *you* want, I'll respect that, but it's certainly not what I'm requesting. I don't look at you and think *platonic*. Not even a little bit."

"Oh..." I was glad he couldn't see me because my cheeks were flushing again. Pressing a hand briefly to my chest, I cleared my throat and sat up a little straighter in my seat, gripping the steering wheel tighter. "Well, we'll see. I'll definitely let you know, if that's all right."

"Absolutely. Whenever you're ready."

I went on about my lunch hour, trying and failing to push Kingston's invitation out of my mind. It *was* refreshing to know up front what his intentions were, as far as why he wanted to see me. And I didn't find myself doubting his sincerity.

When I got a couple of texts from him after lunchtime, I shook my head and tucked my phone back into my pocket, deciding to address them later. He really was laying it on thick.

Before I left for the day, I made sure to stop and poke my head in on Ms. Corine. Didn't expect to see her sitting there closely inspecting her wig, her thin natural hair in neat cornrows that needed to be redone. She looked up when she heard me chuckling.

"What are you doing, Ms. Corine?"

"I keep feeling like something is stickin' me in my head when I have this thing on," she muttered, resuming her inspection. "Might be time for a new one."

"You say that every month. There are at least ten wigs behind you."

"Can never have enough."

"I say the same thing about Oreos. How are you today, other than the poking wig?"

"Just fine. Got my dress all ready for the ball. I'm doing green this year."

"Lovely."

"My man friend will have a matching tie. You have one of those yet?"

"A tie?"

"A man friend."

I had entered the room and started straightening up her bed, since she almost never made it after getting up from her naps. Her question made me pause just long enough to draw an intrigued smirk from her.

Plunking the short brown wig back onto her head, she excitedly turned towards me. "Who is he?"

"There's really nothing to tell, Ms. Corine," I insisted, folding the big blanket she often wrapped around her shoulders as she watched television. "I don't have a man."

"But there's somebody you want, though. Somebody you're interested in. And don't try to lie; you looked struck when I asked about it. So quit acting shy and spill it."

She wasn't going to let up about this and I knew it. "He's *not* my man," I made sure to specify first, placing the folded blanket neatly at the foot of her bed. "But if I'm honest about it...yes, there is someone I have a little bit of interest in."

"And he likes you too, right?"

"So he says."

"So what's the problem?"

"Don't know him all that well. Still feeling him out. And trying to decide if I even want to be bothered."

"Hmph, I don't know why that's even a question. Ain't nothin' like having some companionship from a good man. If they'd let me, I'd have Mr. Murray move right here into this room."

"Mr. Murray? You mean my *boss*, Mr. Murray??"

"I like 'em younger."

Of course, that made me think of Kingston. I had temporarily forgotten that he was twelve years my junior.

"This guy is a little younger than me, too," I admitted.

"So what you worried about? What folks are gonna think?"

"No, no; it's got nothing to do with that. It's like I said, I'm just not sure I want to bother with anybody. I haven't exactly been hitting it out of the park when it comes to men these past few years; I feel like I've run out of energy for the whole process."

"You really wanna spend your life alone?" Ms. Corine challenged, leaning forward slightly and looking right into my eyes. "Because you're scared of getting your feelings hurt again?"

My automatic instinct was to dispute that, but she wasn't wrong. I had managed to convince myself that I would be satisfied with just my son, friends, work, and occasional ill-advised dairy. Figured the memories from my marriage with Nate would be enough for me to savor indefinitely.

But that wasn't enough and I knew it. Now that I had thawed a little from that whole thing with Bradley, I knew that deep down, I really *did* want companionship. Of the romantic variety.

Just like I knew deep down that I was interested in Kingston. And it was silly to pretend like I wasn't.

So when I got home a couple of hours later, I called him.

"I was just about to call and see if you'd made it home yet," he said upon answering. "How's it going, Adele?"

"All is well," I replied, mindlessly shifting my weight from side to side and rubbing my hip. "I'm not disturbing you from anything, am I?"

"Not at all. I love that you're calling me."

"Yeah?"

"Absolutely. Unless of course you're calling with some bad news, like you don't want to hear from me anymore or just want to keep things on the friendship tip."

What a table turn that would be, huh? Me actually friend-zoning someone?

"That's not why I'm calling," I informed him, my voice lowered a bit. "I, um...I was going to let you know that I *do* want to go out with you. On a date. That is, if the offer from earlier still stands."

"Hell yeah, it still stands!" Kingston exclaimed, and I couldn't help but grin. "And here I was wondering if I had run you off by being too eager or something. I'm glad to hear that's not the case."

"Kingston, I'm willing to see what comes of this," I hedged, playing with the hem of my shirt. "But that thing you said before about patience? I hope you meant that. Because I'm sure I'll be testing it at some point."

"That's life, sweetheart. No doubt I'll test yours at some point, too, but hopefully we both remember to see stuff for what it is in the moment and just deal with it, without blowing it up. You work with me, I'll work with you."

"Very easy to say going in. But valid points. In the meantime, though, let's just focus on this first date and go from there."

"Sounds good to me."

Chapter 7

THIS NIGHT CAME MUCH too quickly.

I was trying to keep myself calm as I got ready for my first date with Kingston. It didn't make sense for me to be so nervous; I should've been the queen of first dates by that point. But there I was, with shaking hands and a swirling gut.

Christopher poked his head in as I pressed my hand to my stomach.

"Aww, Ma. What did you eat?"

"What? I haven't eaten anything."

"You're holding your stomach like you do after you eat some ice cream or something else you're not supposed to have."

"I'd *love* some ice cream right now. But that's not the case this time."

He ventured further into my room, glancing at all the discarded outfits on my bed. Several pairs of shoes were scattered over the cream carpeting.

"You nervous or something, Ma?"

I looked at him through the mirror on my vanity as I put on my dangly earrings. "What makes you think that?"

"Zuri does this same thing when she's freaking out about a debate or recital she's nervous about."

I whipped around in my seat. "How do you know that? When were you in her room??"

"Facetime, Ma."

"Oh."

"I haven't even been to her house yet; she's usually doing something after school," Christopher informed me, perching on the edge of my bed. "But she wanted me to ask you if she could come over here one day soon. Said it was time the two of you met."

"So, what, y'all are official now?"

"According to her. But I'll go along with it since I actually *do* like her."

"You have a lot to learn about romance, son."

"So I guess we're *both* in a relationship now, huh, Ma?"

"No," I quickly retorted. "I can't claim that yet. This is just our first date."

"What's the guy's name that you're going out with?"

Hesitating slightly, I replied, "Kingston."

"Wish I had a cool name like that. You gave me one of the most basic, boring names ever. Even Zuri mentioned it."

"Well, she's entitled to her opinion," I muttered, even though I was already starting not to like this little heffah. She sure seemed to have a lot to say.

Deciding that I looked as good as I was going to look, I stood and grabbed the pair of nude pumps I had finally decided on.

"You look nice, Ma," Christopher informed me with a smile.

"Thanks, baby."

"You gonna be out late?"

"I'll be back when I get back. Don't get any ideas about having that new girlfriend of yours come here while I'm gone. Or anybody else, for that matter, outside of your Auntie Rashida. Or your granddad."

"Granddad never comes over here."

"Just giving you the full list, for the record." I went over and kissed his forehead. "See you later. Love you."

"Have a good time, Ma. Love you, too. And no dairy."

"I have no idea what you're talking about."

I had initially opted to just meet Kingston, but he managed to convince me to let him pick me up. I thought we'd be doing the typical first date thing; go get some dinner and then whatever throw-in activity came after that, which for most men was a movie.

But apparently, Kingston wanted to show he wasn't like most men.

"Is this an ice skating rink??"

"Yep." He grinned at me as he put the car in park and undid his seatbelt. "Weren't expecting this, huh?"

"Not even a little bit."

"I told you to be ready for anything."

"Yeah, but I thought you meant some strange kind of cuisine where they make stuff out of unusual animal parts or where you have to eat on the floor. *Not* ice skating."

"You don't like ice skating?"

"Never done it."

"Then it'll be a new experience for both of us. Come on."

Warily, I got out of the car and let Kingston lead me into the ice skating rink (by hand). I felt a little ridiculous in my black dress that clearly wasn't meant for the occasion. Kingston was wearing dark jeans and a chest-hugging v-neck sweater, so at least I had that to ogle while I tried not to make a fool of myself.

"Just so you know, we're totally over if I break any bones out here," I warned after he got our skates. We sat on a nearby bench.

He glanced at me, trying to see if I was kidding or not. I kinda wasn't. "I wouldn't let anything happen to you."

"I have no idea what I'm doing, Kingston."

"That's the case with a lot of people out here. Nobody's expecting Olympian skill, babe; it's just fun."

Something shot through me at the *babe* thing. It still felt strange to hear a man call me that; Kingston had said it a few times since I agreed to date him and it still made me pause. Not that I hated it; it just tripped me out to hear it again. And from a man as yummy as Kingston.

"I guess," I muttered, lacing up my skates.

Once we were in our skates and had secured my purse in one of the lockers, Kingston led me to the rink. There were quite a few people out there, mostly families and a few people looking like they were putting on some kind of performance for whoever. I didn't see any other couples on dates, which made me feel even sillier. But I told myself to chill out and just try to enjoy Kingston's company.

Taking my hands, Kingston stepped onto the ice first before helping me on, glancing over his shoulder before slowly gliding backwards. My legs wobbled as I looked down at my feet, still not believing my non-athletic ass was out there.

"Don't look down; just look at me," Kingston instructed, squeezing my hands gently.

When I looked up at his face, his lips were curved into an encouraging smile, which eased my nerves a little bit. I tried not to think about the fact that I was trying to balance all this weight on a blade of metal on top of ice and just focus on those brown eyes of his. The fact that he didn't have any more experience with this than I did was irrelevant; I still felt safe with him guiding me.

"I'm glad you're here," he told me. "And thank you for wearing that dress."

"If I'd known we'd be doing this, I'd have worn something a little more appropriate."

"Who said it's inappropriate? You're not wearing a ball gown."

"That would be worse, I guess, huh?"

"Much. Not that I'd be any less inclined to claim you."

"Oh, right. If I came out here dressed like Ms. America, you'd probably leave me to struggle on my own while you went and got your whirl-on, telling me to just meet you at the car later."

"That wouldn't be very gentlemanly of me. Though I *would* encourage you to lose the tiara."

"No tiara? Might be a deal breaker."

While we were talking about this foolishness, I noticed we had almost done a lap already. I wasn't feeling quite as shaky and wobbly as I was before and figured I could manage to stay upright on my own, but Kingston wasn't trying to let go of my hands. So we just continued our slow glide around the rink, being sure to stay off to the side and out of the way of the more experienced skaters out there. We picked up speed a little bit but then I started feeling myself a little too much and tried balancing on one leg, thinking I was Kristi Yamaguchi or somebody. Wobble city. Straight lost my balance and fell into Kingston's arms.

"I've got you, babe," he assured me, his arms tight around my waist.

"Thank-"

My breath hitched when I looked up and realized how close our faces were. He was giving me a look that brought the quivers back to my legs, though I knew it had nothing to do with the cold in the rink or my being an ice skating novice.

His eyes dropped to my lips; my eyes dropped to his. When he licked his bottom lip, my hands automatically clenched around his biceps, taking first notice of their strength. I wondered if he was going to kiss me, then I wondered if I *wanted* him to kiss me.

Oh who was I kidding; of course I did.

But I certainly wasn't about to make the first move. I needed him to do it. And a slow ache started to spread over my body the more I anticipated feeling those lips. I didn't even realize we had stopped moving and were just standing there staring at each other. His cologne, his hands on my body; I became hyper-aware of all of it as our surroundings faded into nothing.

His head was just beginning to lower towards mine when we heard a chorus of giggles next to us.

"They're gonna make out," a teenage blonde girl observed, as her and her friends watched us in anticipation.

Kingston cleared his throat and I adjusted my glasses as we separated slightly. I cut my eyes at the girls, who hurriedly skated away.

"You good?" Kingston asked, his hand still on my waist.

I briefly pressed a hand to my chest, willing my heart to stop thumping. "Yeah, I'm fine."

"You, um…" He rubbed the back of his neck. "You want to do a few more laps or are you ready to pack it in?"

"I…guess we can keep at it for a little longer." My hand was still gripping his shirt. "But you're feeding me after this, right?"

"Of course."

We stayed at the rink a while longer, the awkwardness of our interrupted first kiss slowly easing. Kingston made me forget all the discomfort I'd felt when we first got there, making me laugh and keeping me engaged in smooth conversation. Part of me wondered if he'd try that kiss again at some point before the night was over with, but I nudged the thought to the back of my mind. I admittedly didn't have the nerve to ask him that.

When we'd finally had our fill of ice skating, we gathered our things and headed out. We walked closely without touching and I enjoyed the light brushes of my arm against his. Then he gently grabbed my forearm, sliding his hand down to mine. There went that internal heater again, that seemed to flare whenever he touched me. I wondered if he could feel the dampness in my palms as we continued to walk to his car.

We went to grab something to eat, with still no mention of our little heated moment on the ice. Not that I wasn't still playing mental images of how our kiss would've been in the back of my mind. In fact, the more I thought about it, the more I wanted it to happen.

I just hoped like hell he wanted the same thing I did. And with the heated glances he kept shooting my way and seemingly purposeful brushes of his leg against mine under the table, it felt that chances were pretty good that he did.

"You enjoy yourself, babe?" he asked me as we headed back to my house.

"I really did. It's been a while since I had this much fun."

"Glad to hear it."

"And to think my good time actually involved ice skating."

He chuckled. "It's good to try something new every now and then. And that was a first for the both of us."

"Two ice skating virgins..." My voice trailed off when I realized what I'd said. It hadn't been intended in a sexual way at all, but just the mere mention had me picturing Kingston emerging from a steam-filled bathroom wearing nothing but a towel around his waist and his bottom lip between his teeth. The image had me shifting in my seat, pressing my thighs together and clearing my throat.

Kingston glanced over at me as if he knew what was going through my head. His eyes swept over my body before going back to the road. I noticed his grip on the steering wheel tighten.

"Breaking each other in," he drawled, finishing my quip. His free hand eased closer to my thigh but he apparently caught himself and rested it on the gear shift instead.

"Right." I licked my lips and looked out the window, shifting in my seat again. Now the image of Kingston's bare body that I hadn't even seen yet was stuck in my head. Even though I was no virgin and figured Kingston wasn't either, the thought of us *breaking each other in* was amazingly titillating. The man hadn't even touched me and my body was singing.

Goodness, what's gonna happen if – when- we actually do *go there?* I mused to myself as we turned on the street to my house. I prayed my nipples weren't poking through my dress like it felt like they were. *If he has me like this without even doing anything, actually going to bed with him would probably paralyze me.*

"Here we are," Kingston announced, pulling into my driveway. He glanced at me and rubbed his hands on his thighs.

"Yep." I ran a hand through my locs. "Here we are."

I could feel him looking at me, and I made myself return the gesture. His eyes bore into mine before roaming over my face, his breathing deepening slightly. He wanted to kiss me; I knew it. And the feeling was definitely mutual. With every second that ticked by, the anticipation sent the tingles scurrying over my body further and further into overdrive.

"I don't wanna keep you," he finally said, his voice a little hoarse. He cleared his throat. "I mean, I *do*, but I know you have to get up in the morning..."

"Yeah," I reluctantly admitted. "And I'd invite you in, but my son is in there and I'm not quite ready for you two to meet yet..."

"Hey, I get it," he assured me with a quick wave of his hand. "I totally respect that. When I get to meet your son is your call. I'll just walk you to the door."

I didn't bother telling him he didn't have to do that because I wanted him to do it. There was a large part of me that wasn't quite ready for the evening to end yet, but figured it was probably better to quit while I was ahead.

Kingston took my hand as he helped me out of the car, and held onto it as we casually strolled up the driveway to the front door. Both of our heads were tilted towards the ground, our hands mildly swinging back and forth in rhythm with our steps.

"Thank you for letting me take you out, Adele," he said. He looked up at me slightly as I stepped up onto the stone step in front of the door. His hand was still gripping mine. "I hope this is just the first of many, though."

"I hope so, too," I allowed myself to admit. I eyed him from behind my glasses, actually wishing I didn't have to wear the damn things for once. "Thank you for a great evening."

"My pleasure." He stepped a little closer. "I already can't wait until we can do it again."

"Me, either."

"Good." His eyes sparkled under the light over the door. "There's something else I can't wait to do..."

Although I had an idea, I asked anyway. "What's that?"

"Kiss you." His hand slid up my arm, stopping at my elbow. "Please tell me I can kiss you now, Adele."

Hell yeah, you can. "Yes."

Wasting no time, he stepped closer, leaning up and brushing his lips against mine. The light stuff only lasted for a moment, though, before we each opened our mouths to each other, giving in. He gripped my waist as my hands slid around his shoulders, leaning into him as I let myself totally melt, whimpering in surrender. His kiss was slow, deep, and deliberate, the kind I loved.

He stepped up onto the step and backed me against the door, the kiss never breaking and his arms tightening around my waist. Arousal thumped through my body like bass through speakers, his occasional moans and grunts only turning up the volume. My leg rubbed against his, wanting to be closer to him and temporarily forgetting that we were out in the open in full view of my neighbors. I didn't care. I was too consumed with the feel of Kingston's tongue stroking mine, his hard body under my hands and his hands roaming my back and sliding teasingly close to my ass, his orgasmic cologne, and the way my body was aching almost to the point of pain.

Before I lost my head and invited him up to my bedroom, I made myself ease away. I tried to gather myself as Kingston rested his forehead against mine, each of us trying to catch our breath from our surprisingly intense first kiss.

"Damn, woman," he whispered, one of his hands grasping the back of my neck and the other gripping the side of my face. His breathing was still deep and heavy, just like mine, and his jaw clenched with forced restraint.

"Right back at ya."

Several more moments passed with neither of us saying anything. His hands slid down to my shoulders and arms before linking his fingers with mine. As much as I knew I should probably get on in the house, I was in no hurry to end this moment we were having.

"I'll call you," he finally breathed, his voice a little gruff.

I nodded, my lips already missing his. "Okay."

His hand came up to grab my face again and he gave me a look that hinted he wanted to lay another one on me, but he just bit his lip before giving me a lingering kiss on the cheek and a slow peck to the lips. He stepped back.

"Good night, babe."

I adjusted my glasses and plastered a hand to my chest. I knew my cheeks were flushed. "Good night, Kingston."

He continued to stand there and I realized he was waiting for me to go inside the house. Managing to find my keys in my purse and unlock the front door with shaky hands, I waved at him before gently closing the door, turning and leaning against it as I let out a long breath. I heard his car door close and his engine start up, and resisted the urge to go to the window and watch him drive off like a longing puppy. Our kiss was already replaying through my mind as the sound of his car faded into the night.

Actually fanning myself, I willed myself to calm down so I could make my way up the stairs. That date had gone way better than expected.

And when Kingston texted me a half hour later to let me know he'd made it home and that he was already missing me, and the grin automatically shot across my face, I knew I was in big trouble. Because whether I wanted to or not, I missed him already, too.

Chapter 8

KINGSTON AND I HAD been dating for a few weeks, and even though we hadn't had that *are we official?* talk yet, he was surely acting as if we were. More than a couple of times, he referred to me as his woman, either in our own conversations or when we were talking to others, like the server at a restaurant or the friends he had already introduced me to. I didn't call him on it because, well...dammit, I liked hearing it. Yeah, there was the tiny part of me that felt we were moving a little fast, but I went against my natural inclination and ignored that.

Simply put, I was into Kingston. *Really* into him. So much so that it kinda scared me. And that fear helped me to not look too far ahead and just enjoy things as they were.

I still hadn't let him meet Christopher yet, and to my surprise, he wasn't pestering me about it. He had apparently meant it when he said it was my call. Christopher wanted to meet Kingston, though, and repeatedly asked what was taking me so long to make the introduction. He didn't get what the big deal was, since I usually met his girlfriends pretty quickly. (Still hadn't met Zuri, though, who he was still with, surprisingly). I had to try to explain to him why my meeting his girlfriend and him meeting my...meeting Kingston wasn't the same thing.

Kingston and I *had* hung out with Rashida and her new man, Jared, though, and it only gave her more fuel in her mission to get Kingston and I down the aisle. I let her know she was *majorly* jumping the gun with that, but she swore she could see it happening. Thankfully, she never said anything about this in front of Kingston. No need in freaking the man out now that I'd finally allowed myself to open up to him. Well, for the most part.

When Kingston called me one morning as I was getting ready for work, I looked at my phone in amazement. He had been unpredictably consistent with the calls, ringing my phone damn near every morning before work, before we went to bed, with several texts in between during the day. I had expected that to taper off by then, but it hadn't. Just like he was still being a sweetheart and showering me with compliments and acting like I was the hottest thing walking. Super flattering, but it had to be only a matter of time before he got tired of doing all that. Right?

And of course (and thank *god*) he was still laying those bone-melting kisses on me.

"I cannot believe I'm making out on the couch like some teenager," I murmured between kisses as Kingston started sucking on my neck. I writhed against him, not wanting to admit he found one of my spots.

"I'm just glad that Christopher is off at that basketball tournament," he whispered, apparently discovering that he had hit paydirt and going for the spot again, moaning when I moaned. "It's about time we gave your spot some action."

Gently pushing against his shoulders, I reared back slightly. "And just what kind of *action* do you think you're about to get right now?"

He tsked. "Chill out, woman; I'm talking about doing what we're doing now. I know we're not taking it *there* yet." He ran a hand over my stomach and my own hand immediately landed on top of his, wanting to remove it but not wanting to have to explain why. Especially since he had certainly felt me up plenty by then.

Licking those lips, he leisurely ran his gaze down my body before returning his eyes to mine. "May I continue?"

"Please do."

We resumed our making out, with Kingston eventually ending up on top of me on the couch. My jaw fell open as he kissed down my neck and teasingly close to my breasts and back up again. It was another moment that I kind of regretted telling him that we should wait a while before having sex, because I surely wanted him right then.

I wanted Kingston period. Way more than I wanted to.

The thing that was jumbling my mind was that I couldn't figure out why a young(er) stud like Kingston would be so enamored with *me*. I didn't think badly of myself at all, but I wasn't delusional, either. Most people wouldn't match the two of us together. Hell, *I* surely wouldn't have.

The man actually told me he could see himself falling hard for me. And that had me stumped like someone had lobbed a history question at me on *Jeopardy*.

In my mind, none of this made sense. And until I made some sense *of* it, I just didn't want to get my hopes up about anything.

But I felt I was already in deeper than I wanted to be. I hadn't felt that way about anyone since Nate. How had I gone from zero to sixty that quickly?

It was something that was constantly on my mind; after Christopher returned from his tournament, when I was on the phone with Rashida, assembling puzzles with Dad, or doing my half-ass workouts at the gym. I didn't know what it was about Kingston that was so different than the other men I dated since Nate. It wasn't like he was the first man to show me any real interest; despite my constant bellyaching about not being looked at romantically by men, there *were* a couple of instances over the years since Nate passed where I was the dump-*er* instead of the dump-*ee*. So I wasn't desperate.

I went from not even wanting to be bothered to Kingston being damn near all I could think about. And as good as it felt, I couldn't say I loved that.

THE ONLY THING THAT managed to get my mind off of Kingston for a while was work. More specifically, the crappy day I was having *at* work.

Nothing was going right. My computer crashed. There was an ant issue in the employee break room. Not one but two residents had to be rushed to the emergency room. Some guests who were there to celebrate their father's birthday almost got to fighting. I broke a nail.

It was a rare day that even going to see Ms. Corine didn't make me feel any better. Not that I had much time to do that, anyway, with everything going on. By the time the day was over with, all I wanted to do was get home, change into some sweats, and hang out with Christopher until I konked out.

But that plan went out the window as soon as I got home.

"Ma, can I spend the night at Dylan's tonight?" Christopher asked as soon as I trudged through the front door.

"He's having a few of us from the team over; gonna have a gaming marathon."

"A gaming marathon, huh?" I tried to hide my disappointment as he followed me up to my room. Kicking my shoes off, I glanced over at him as he leaned against the doorjamb. Was he bulking up? He was suddenly looking more muscular than usual. "Sounds like fun."

"So I can go? Dylan's dad said they can pick me up since they're already out."

As much as I had been looking forward to winding my night down with my son, I knew it wouldn't have been fair to make him stay home with me just because I didn't have any other plans. I remembered what Rashida and Dad always told me about not depending on Christopher for company.

"Is your homework done?"

"Yes ma'am."

"Need me to check anything?"

"I'm good. Zuri helped me with the hard stuff in study hall."

"Hmm. Well, that's fine, then. I can fix you something to eat before you leave, if you give me a minute..."

"No need. They had five dollar pizzas after school and me and Zuri shared one. That'll hold me 'til I get to Dylan's."

"I see." I pretended to be occupied with getting my earrings off as I tried to ignore the pang of not being needed. "Have fun. Just make sure you've straightened up your room and gotten all the trash out."

"Already done. Thanks, Ma." He pushed off the doorjamb and disappeared down the hall, actually whistling.

With a deep sigh, I told myself that I had no reason to be upset or to take anything personally. Christopher was just being a typical teenager; of course he wanted to hang with his friends on a Friday night instead of sitting around the house with me.

Grabbing my phone, I hit the button for Rashida's number as I rummaged through my laundry basket full of clean but unfolded clothes for my favorite pair of sweats.

"What's up, girl?" Rashida answered. Music was playing in the background.

"Hey; you partying or something?"

"Not yet. But gimme a couple of hours."

"Oh, you're going out?" I asked with a slump of the shoulders.

"Yeah, Jared should be here in about a half hour or so. And lord knows I'm looking forward to getting loose with him tonight after the day from hell I had."

"You too? I was hoping we could hang out but I guess that's shot now."

"I'm sorry, girl. You know I love you but tonight I need the kind of tension relief you can't give me."

"Hmph. Well, I guess I'll find something to do. Christopher won't be here; he's going to Dylan's in a little bit."

"Why aren't you spending the evening with Kingston? Where is he?"

"I don't know...we've exchanged a few texts today but haven't had much chance to talk. There was just too much going on at work, from my end. I'm not sure what he's doing tonight, actually."

"Well, call and ask him. Invite him over so you can have some of your own tension relief. 'Cause it sure sounds like you need it."

I didn't want to tell Rashida that I was still pondering so much about my budding relationship with Kingston, and wanted to keep my distance until I figured it all out. All she would say was that the fact that this was even an issue must've meant that Kingston was something special, and that I shouldn't analyze things so much and just enjoy it. And maybe she was right. But my mind was too jumbled and until I un-jumbled it, I was no good to anybody.

"I guess," I replied, agreeing to nothing. "He's probably busy, anyway. I'll just take a shower, order some takeout, pluck out a few chin hairs and find something good to watch on TV."

"What fun you are," Rashida muttered.

"Girl, as drained as I am, I don't have the energy to try to be fun."

"I still think you should call Kingston. Invite him over and spend the evening cuddled up on the couch. I bet he could make you feel better."

I bet he could, too. "What was that you said before about not depending on other people for company?"

"You know good and well I was talking about your son, not your man." I could hear some things knocking around in the background, and I knew she was rummaging through her makeup case. I'd seen her getting-dolled-up routine enough to know. "Why are you hesitating like you don't want to see him? You two have a fight or something?"

"No, no, nothing like that. That answer would require more time than you have. But I'm not upset with him at all."

"Hmm. Good. And at least if Kingston is there, you won't eat any ice cream or grilled cheese sandwiches or something else you're not supposed to eat."

I sucked my teeth as I pulled some yoga pants and a t-shirt from the laundry basket; my sweats must have still been in my gym bag. "Please, I have a little more self-control than that."

"No, you don't. But anyway, I need to go; Jared will be here in a minute and I still need to run a flat iron through this hair and get my dress on."

"All right. Well, you two have fun."

"Oh, we will. And Adele?"

"What?"

"Call Kingston."

She hung up before I could respond. Truth was, I wouldn't have minded seeing Kingston. But I didn't know if I'd be able to hide the fact that so much was weighing on my mind. And this wasn't something I was gung-ho talking to him about, even though he played a pretty major role in the answer. I guess I just felt that if I flat-out asked why he was so into *me* of all people, he'd just tell me something he thought I'd want to hear, even though he seemed to be pretty straight up about things so far.

But when I stopped to think about it, how else *would* I find that out unless I asked him?

I was making all of this harder than it had to be, and I knew it. I had never been this scattered over a man before; my self-assurance had always been something I was rather proud of, whether my stance was right or wrong. But Kingston had me all over the place, and I wasn't sure that was a good thing.

Christopher left a little while later, and I tried to decide what I was going to order for dinner as I went about doing some light cleaning around the house. I needed to keep myself occupied, even though I was tired. Part of me *did* wonder what Kingston was up to, but I didn't have to wonder long because he called.

"Hey, babe," he greeted. "What's going on?"

"Hey..." I still wasn't to the level of pet names yet. "Not too much. Just straightening up a little bit right now."

"I hate we didn't get to talk much today but it was crazy at work. So glad to be done."

"Seems to be going around. My work day sucked, too."

"How 'bout we make each other feel better, then. I can come hang with you, or we can go out somewhere. Is Christopher around?"

"Uh, no, he's at a friend's house tonight."

"Nice. Have you eaten yet? I can bring you something."

I couldn't resist a small smile. "You know those are magic words."

"Of course I do. What do you want? I can grab it and be on my way within the hour."

My mouth was all fixed to say yes, then I looked down and remembered the wrinkled t-shirt I was wearing and the leggings that were covering unshaved legs.

"Damn...okay, see this is the un-cute part about dating me..." I hedged.

"I don't get it..."

"I'm not exactly presentable. My locs need re-twisting, I've been cleaning the house, I need a pedicure, my legs are probably hairier than yours-"

"You think I care about any of that, Adele?"

"*I* care."

"Most of that could be fixed in the time it'll take me to get over there, but regardless, I just want to wind this night down with my woman. I'm not worried about that superficial bullshit."

"Easy to say that over the phone."

"You doubting me now?"

This would have been a good opening to let him know that there were some things on my mind regarding our relationship. But when I opened my mouth to broach the subject, I couldn't find the right words.

"I guess I *am* being silly," I finally conceded, mentally kicking myself. "Of course you can come over. And some Jamaican food would be much appreciated."

"I got you, babe. Same order as usual or something else?"

"The usual. Not in the mood to be adventurous."

He chuckled. "Damn, I love talking to you. All right, I'll be there in about an hour or so. Hopefully it won't be much longer than that but I still need to change and you know our Jamaican spot is gonna be crowded, with it being Friday night and all."

"It's fine. I'm not going anywhere."

"And those are *my* magic words." I could hear the smile in his voice, which had dropped an octave. All of a sudden I couldn't wait to see him. Damn it. "I'll text you when I'm headed that way."

We ended the call and I blew out a shaky breath. I needed to get myself together, in more ways than one.

I rushed upstairs to un-grungify myself, but as I was stripping off my wrinkled and now slightly dusty t-shirt and shaking out my locs, I stopped. Suddenly I didn't feel it was necessary to pretty up for Kingston. He had already said he didn't care what I had on. And I was a little curious as to how he would react and behave when he actually saw me; it was one thing to insist that how I looked didn't make any difference over the phone, but quite another to get cuddly with someone who looked like they'd been stranded on an island without beauty products.

So the only things I allowed myself to do in preparation for Kingston's arrival was brush my teeth, wash my face, put on a clean t-shirt and some socks to cover my un-pedicured feet, and finish straightening up the living room. A teeny-tiny voice kept reminding that I still had time to get another quick shower, run a razor over my legs and put on something casual-cute. But I had already turned this into a test of Kingston's sincerity, and I was looking forward to his reaction to my appearance almost as much as I was looking forward to seeing him.

Finally, he texted to let me know he was ten minutes away, and I resisted the urge again to run upstairs.

"*Really* need to chill out," I admonished myself, dropping defiantly into the armchair. "This will be good; I need to see how he reacts when things are less than ideal."

I had talked myself into this rationale, but when he arrived and I opened the door to see him standing there looking sexy as *fuck* while smiling and armed with my favorite cuisine, I did the only thing I could do.

Slammed the door in his face.

Chapter 9

"WHAT'S GOING ON, ADELE?"

I already felt stupid, standing there against the door while he was probably thinking I'd lost my mind. Here I had told the man he could come over and then I shut him out as soon as he gets there.

Momentarily squeezing my eyes shut, I made myself open the door. He was looking at me with what looked to be a mix of concern and frustration. Couldn't blame him for that because I was damn frustrated with myself, too.

"I'm sorry about that, Kingston...you can come on in."

He eyed me warily as I stepped back so he could come inside. Once he was finally across the threshold, he asked, "What's up with that?"

Pushing the door closed and locking it, I figured I might as well be real about it.

"You came here looking all delicious and here I am looking like somebody's 'before' picture."

"What?" Kingston put the bags of food on the coffee table and turned to me. I noticed he had yet to fully take a head-to-toe perusal of me; his eyes had remained on my face. Pulling me to him, he gave me a soft kiss on the lips. "You're still on that, babe?"

"Well...I'd managed to make myself forget about it but then you come up in here with gray sweatpants on and that tight shirt, looking like an orgasm with legs. Not to mention smelling like deliciousness..."

He chuckled, actually looking like he was blushing a little bit. I could see the faint dimple in his cheek and I automatically wanted to run my tongue across it.

"I'm glad you're pleased," he commented, holding me tighter. "And before you ask, I am, too."

His words warmed me. "You haven't even really looked at me yet."

"I *am* looking at you," he retorted, his eyes fixed on mine. "And I see everything I need to see."

Now I was hot. What in the world was this man doing to me?

Before I could think too much about it, he leaned in and claimed my lips, his strong hand sliding to the middle of my back and pressing me closer. I allowed myself to get lost in his lips, melting into him and enjoying the feeling of his hard body under my hands. His long tongue leisurely stroked against mine, taking his time and sending pleasure pings to every inch of my body. That tongue was dangerous.

"We should probably go ahead and eat, huh?" he eventually muttered against my lips before gently nipping my chin.

Usually I was all for the eating but in that moment, the food in those bags on my coffee table was the last thing on my mind. I just wanted Kingston to keep doing what he was doing to my lips. But I made myself agree. "I suppose, yeah."

After stealing a few more pecks, Kingston stepped back and went to take the food out of the bags. I resisted the urge to fan my flushed face as I scurried to the kitchen to get some plates. After we dished up the food, we parked it on the couch and dug in. I tried to conceal the smile that wanted to break out when he sat really close to me.

"I swear, I've been thinking about this oxtail all week," he insisted, briefly closing his eyes in appreciation as he chewed. "If I could eat these bad boys every day, I would."

"You could probably get away with it. If I tried that, I'd be as big as a house."

"You're a trip, you know that?"

"I've heard similar feedback."

"My mom makes some bangin' oxtail; that's how I fell in love with 'em."

Briefly cutting my eyes at him, I stuffed a plantain into my mouth. "Oh yeah?"

"Mmm-hmm." He wiped his mouth with a napkin. "Do you make these?"

"I have once or twice but I don't bother too much, since Christopher never really cared for them."

"Buddy doesn't know what he's missing. But to keep it real, there really wasn't anything that my mama cooked that I didn't love. Nothing like a woman that can cook." He winked at me. "Like you."

My back stiffened slightly. "Well, we've gotta eat and I don't want my son living on pizza and wings, so..."

"Sounds like me in college. Mama used to send me care packages every month to make sure I ate decent stuff at least some of the time."

I wasn't sure why we were talking about his mother so much.

"Mothers do that kind of thing. Um, *anyway*," I adjusted my glasses. "You know one thing I realized I don't know about you? What hobbies you have."

"Really? We haven't talked about that? Well, don't clown me for this, but I actually like making pottery."

My fork clanked against my plate as I turned to him in pleasant surprise. "*Shut* up, for real?"

"I told you not to clown me."

"I'm not; I actually think that's cool. It's one of those things I've always kinda wanted to do but never did anything about it."

"You should try it sometime; I bet you'd like it."

"You'll have to show me some of your creations."

"I can, yeah, but they're not very good. I kinda suck at it. I just enjoy it because it's relaxing and a fun creative outlet. Even if it does look like something a kindergartener made."

"I bet it's not that bad. It can't be any worse than my attempts at drawing."

"You'll see the next time you come over. Mama still teases me about some of 'em."

I pursed my lips. I hadn't even met Kingston's mama and she was already interfering.

Then a thought slammed into my mind like a linebacker. Was the reason that Kingston was so enamored with me was that I in some way reminded him of his mother? Was that why he kept bringing her up? We'd been dating for weeks and he had mentioned her once or twice, but never *this* much.

He sipped from his bottle of Ting. "You actually kinda remind me of her, come to think of it."

That did it.

"Okay, pause." I set my plate on the coffee table and turned to him. He was looking like he didn't know what was going on.

"What's wrong, babe? Pause what?"

"Verify a couple of things for me first...you're an only child, right?"

"Yeah..."

"And your mama lives out of state, right?"

"Yeah..."

"And she was a single mother, right? It was just the two of you?"

He frowned slightly. "Where are you going with this, Adele?"

"Where I'm going is to the realization that you only want to be with me because I remind you of your mama. And if that's the case, I'm *not* flattered."

His frown deepened as he set his own plate down. "What are you talking about?"

"Why are you with me, Kingston?" I blurted, shooting off the couch. "What is it that you see in me that keeps you coming around so much? I was beginning to flatter myself into thinking that maybe you actually *were* sincerely just attracted to me *as me* but now I'm starting to wonder. Is it because I'm like your mother?"

He looked up at me a moment before standing. In a voice calmer than mine, he replied, "Actually, you two *do* have a lot in common."

My jaw dropped. I wasn't expecting him to actually admit it. Hell, I had been hoping I was wrong.

In the next second, though, I felt myself actually start quivering with anger. I didn't need this. Clamping my mouth shut, I stalked over to the door.

"What are you doing?" He was right on my heels.

"I already have a son," I reminded him bitingly. "And I damn sure don't need another one."

"What??"

"You need to go, Kingston."

"Adele-"

"We don't have anything else to talk about."

"I think we *do*," he insisted, closing the door before I could fully open it. "Because we're *clearly* not on the same page, here."

"Yes, I've already figured that out, thank you. I am not interested in being some kind of weird lover-maternal hybrid for you. If that's what you're into, that's your business, but you're gonna have to find it somewhere else. I'm not the one."

"Will you please let me talk??"

"For what? So you can try to tell me I'm crazy and that it was a total coincidence that you kept bringing up your mama every two seconds? I love my father plenty but you don't hear me talking about him on dates."

"Adele." He reached above me to push the door closed again. "Can we just please take a beat and talk about this rationally? You've got it all wrong!"

"Do I? Because I've been wracking my brain trying to figure out why someone twelve years my junior and hot enough to be in somebody's underwear ad would be so into *me*, and now I *finally* have an answer that makes sense. So I guess I should thank you for clearing up that confusion. At least I'm not deluding myself anymore."

"Adele!"

I managed to yank open the door just in time to see a car pull into the driveway. When Christopher stepped out of the backseat, I cursed under my breath, closing the door quickly.

"What's wrong?" Kingston asked, taking a step towards me, his dark brows bunched in concern.

"My son came home early," I grumbled. "Dammit!"

"Can we finish this conversation later? Because I'm not trying to leave things like this, Adele."

That wasn't the main thing on my mind anymore; now I was frustrated because I was going to be forced to introduce Kingston to Christopher, and I hadn't planned on doing that just yet. Well, not that it mattered much at that point, anyway, since Kingston and I were clearly over.

"Would you mind grabbing your stuff and running out the back real quick?" I hissed with a quick peek out of the window by the door.

Kingston gave me a look like he couldn't believe my nerve and folded his arms. "Actually yes, I *would* mind."

"Ugh! What about hiding in the bathroom or closet, then?"

"I'm not doing that, Adele."

"Kingston, this is not the time to-"

"Ma?" Christopher called out from the front step. "Are you leaning against the door?"

I sighed, defeated. Might as well get this over with.

Stepping back, I opened the door, forcing a smile onto my face. "Hey, baby...uh, what happened? What are you doing back here? I thought you were staying at Dylan's tonight."

"Yeah, I was, but a pipe busted in their house so it wasn't the best time to be over there." Christopher then noticed Kingston standing there. "Sorry to interrupt your date, Ma."

"Oh, no need to apolo-"

"I'm Christopher," he introduced, going over to Kingston with his hand out. "Are you Kingston?"

"I am." Kingston grasped his hand firmly. "It's nice to finally meet you, man."

"You, too. I've been telling Ma that I wanted to finally see who she was going with but she kept saying that needed to wait."

"Yeah, same here, but it's understandable. You've gotta be careful about who you have around your kids, especially nowadays. She's just trying to watch out for you, that's all."

Nice of him to say. Too bad the timing of this little meetup sucked.

"I guess that makes sense," Christopher admitted. "I've heard some kids at school talk about how many people their parents bring home. They were pretty embarrassed about it. Ma never did anything like that. So I guess the fact that you're here means she must really like you; she doesn't usually bring anybody home."

My face flamed and I didn't dare look at Kingston to see his reaction to that.

"Um, Christopher, if you're hungry, you can have some of my dinner," I quickly interjected. Wanted to stop this conversation before Christopher told Kingston that I had doodled his name on my notebook.

(Actually it was just an old takeout menu and it was *one* time while I was waiting on my roast to finish).

"Oh, no thanks, Ma," Christopher replied, peering over at our half-eaten plates. "You know I'm not too crazy about Jamaican food. We ate at Dylan's before the pipe thing happened. I'll just go up to my room and leave y'all alone. Good night, Ma."

Resisting the urge to tell him that wasn't necessary, I accepted his kiss on the cheek. "Good night, baby."

"Nice meeting you, Mr. Kingston."

"You can just call me Kingston, man. And nice meeting you, too."

Christopher trotted up the stairs and we heard his door close. I knew Kingston was looking at me but I kept my eyes on the baseboard.

"Are you willing to hear me out now?" he finally asked.

Taking my time responding, I kept my eyes averted as I said, "I don't think now is the time for that, Kingston." I motioned towards the top of the stairs.

"Yeah, it's a good thing Christopher is here so you have another excuse to avoid listening to me."

My head snapped to him. "That's *not* what I'm doing."

"The hell it's not. Look, babe, I'll leave if you really want me to but not before I set you straight on all this."

"Fine, Kingston." I threw up my hands. "Say what you've gotta say."

"My wanting you has *nothing* to do with my mother. I want you because I'm attracted to you on every level that's important. You've consumed my mind ever since the night we met. I *crave* being around you. You're intelligent and can hold conversations, which isn't as common as it should be nowadays. You make me laugh. You keep me on my toes. And the physical attraction is a whole other conversation because I could talk about that all day." His eyes were as serious as I'd ever seen them as he stepped right in front of me. "I want all of you, for as long as I can have you, Adele. Because you've *got* me."

Damn it. I felt the tears building up behind my glasses. I tried to blink them away but it was a waste of time.

"Do you share some qualities with my mama? Sure," Kingston continued, gently unfolding my arms that I already had forgotten folding and sliding his hands down to mine. "I admire my mother a lot; she's a hell of a woman and so are you. But she has her place in my life and my heart and it's totally separate from yours. There's no overlap."

My earlier anger was melting faster than ice on a scalding skillet. "You're saying I have a place in your heart?"

"Damn right you do," he confirmed with no hesitation. He lifted my hand and placed it on his hard chest. "And that's all about *you*; nobody else. I really hope you believe that."

"Oh, Kingston..."

"And I want you to believe this, too," he continued, taking my face in both of his hands. "You're not pushing me away that easily. Every wall and barrier you have up to guard yourself, I'm busting all those up. I'll say it again; I'm gonna earn your trust, Adele. *And* your heart. It doesn't matter how long it takes. So hopefully this is your last time trying to convince yourself that what's going on here isn't the real thing. Because it *is*."

Before I could respond, he leaned in and kissed me with such intensity that it threw me totally off kilter, backing me against the door. I felt silly but the larger part of me was just plain touched. Kingston's words made me melt even more than his amazing kisses did.

"Do you want me, Adele?" he whispered, nuzzling my cheek. "And I'm not talking about sex. Do you want to be with me? Do you want this to work as much as I do?"

"Yes," I whimpered, unable to say anything else. My mind couldn't think of anything clever or deft, which was usually my superpower. This was one of those times where the *yes* was all that was needed.

"That's all I need – and want – to know." He brought his lips back to mine, gracing me with a few more moments of those pillow-soft lips before slowly stepping back, keeping a hold on my waist. I was actually swaying a little bit. "That's a relief, because I need you to be all in like I am."

"I-I admit I get freaked out at times but it's...it's only because I haven't felt for anyone what I feel for you. Not since my husband died. And I admit, Kingston, that scares me."

"I get it."

"And we're *so* different..."

"We're not that different, babe. But even if we were, that doesn't have to be a bad thing. All that matters is that we want to be together. And there's not a doubt in my mind that I want to be with you."

"I want to be with you, too," I admitted timidly.

"Good. I needed to hear you say that, babe." He leaned in for another kiss before going over and grabbing his keys. "I'm gonna go."

I pushed myself off the door. Even though I had been trying to put him out just a little while before, hearing him actually offer to go unleashed a mild case of panic. "Why?"

"Because our emotions are high right now and I want you to be able to process all of this with a clear head. I'll give you a call tomorrow."

"You don't have to leave, Kingston," I insisted, gingerly putting my hands on his stomach before sliding them around his waist. "As soon as you walk out the door I'll be wishing you could come back, so just save me the trouble and don't go."

A smile eased across his face as his arms encircled me. "You sure?"

"More than sure. And anyway, you didn't finish your oxtail." I grinned up at him, feeling long-dormant swirls of affection roll through my heart. "Wouldn't want those to go to waste, right?"

Returning my grin, he held me tighter and leaned down to steal another kiss, which I gladly gave up. I could get addicted to kissing him. Hell, I already was. The way he used his tongue, how he moved his lips, how he held me and moaned and whispered stuff in my ear...

"You've convinced me," he murmured. "Not that I really wanted to leave, anyway. It's just what I thought you needed me to do."

"I don't. I don't want you to go anywhere."

"Say less, babe."

We stood there holding each other and making out for I don't know how long before we even remembered to get back to our food. When Saturday morning crept in, we were still cuddled on the couch, with me resisting the urge to pinch myself. And Christopher had been locked in his room the whole time.

Best. Date. Ever.

Chapter 10

KINGSTON LEFT EARLY the next morning, wanting to leave before Christopher got up. He had thankfully read my mind, because even though they'd met and Kingston and I had confirmed that we were serious about each other, he was still a stranger to Christopher. And I didn't need to broadcast that my man had spent the night, even though we never left the living room and nothing happened other than kissing and heavy petting.

Wow; that was the first time I thought of Kingston as *my man*. The thought actually made me want to squeal a little bit, as high school as that was.

By the time I cleaned up the living room and took a shower, Christopher was milling around in his room; I could hear his music. He met me down in the kitchen as I started breakfast.

"Morning, Ma."

"Hey, baby. Want some pancakes?"

"Sure. Can you put blueberries in 'em?"

"If we have any left in the refrigerator, yeah. I think you might've eaten 'em all. But I'm pretty sure we have some strawberries, if you want those."

"That'll do. We have any bacon to go with it?"

"You know I keep bacon in here."

He got quiet as I continued to get everything together. My back was to him but I knew he was probably on his phone. Usually I'd say something about him being on that thing so much but this time I was glad for the distraction. If he was focused on that, he'd be less likely to ask me anything about Kingston.

"So Kingston seemed nice."

Guess I should have known better.

"Yeah," I replied casually, stirring the pancake batter. "He really is."

"I like him."

"Really?" I glanced at him in surprise. "You only talked to him for a minute."

"He has a cool vibe. And dope sneakers."

"Doesn't take much to endear you, does it?"

"He looks kinda young. You didn't mention he was younger than you."

My brow quirked. "He's thirty-three. Does him being younger than me bother you?"

"No ma'am. I think it's cool, actually."

"Hmm. Well, good."

"When is he coming back over here? Or did you break up? You didn't break up with him, did you, Ma?"

"No!" I blushed and adjusted my glasses. "No, we didn't break up. I'm sure he'll be back over here soon enough."

"Good. I hope he sticks around, Ma. You really like him; I can tell." Before I could ask how he determined that (as true as it was), his phone chimed and he looked at the message, sucking his teeth.

I frowned. "What's wrong? Who was that?"

"Zuri. She keeps trying to get me to apologize."

"Apologize for what?"

"Because she says I embarrassed her when I met her parents at that debate thing she had the other day. I tripped and accidentally knocked her mama's drink onto her new blouse."

"You didn't say you were sorry when it happened?"

"A few times. Her mama was pretty cool about it. But Zuri wants me to apologize to *her*, since she was so embarrassed. She acts like I tripped on purpose."

"Hmph. Well, that's your girl."

"Since I finally met Kingston, you should finally meet Zuri. She'll have a little more free time since her dad made her quit her job at the mall."

I started to ask why that was, but decided I didn't care. "Sure, yeah, I suppose it *is* time I finally meet this girl who has so much of my baby's attention. We'll set up a time for her to come by."

"Look at us, Ma. Both of us in relationships at the same time," Christopher commented with a smile as he grabbed his phone and turned to leave the room. "Wasn't sure if that was ever gonna happen."

He was out of the room by the time his words registered in my brain. I whirled around from where I'd been rinsing off the strawberries in the sink to hear him whistling in the living room. Resisting the urge to summon him back in there and ask if he was trying to be funny or not, I just told myself to let it go and finish making breakfast.

It didn't take long before my mind forgot about Christopher's words and recalled Kingston's from the night before, and an automatic smile hit my face. With considerably more spring in my step, I bounced over to get the vegetable oil out of the pantry.

"IT'S SUCH A NICE DAY today," Rashida commented as we settled in at one of the stone table-and-bench sets in the Westwood Oaks courtyard the following Monday afternoon.

"Yeah, it is. It's so nice to get outside after being cooped up my office all day." I unwrapped my steak sandwich (Rashida had ignored my cheesesteak request), thanking the lord I didn't do something stupid and get a salad. "Thanks so much for bringing me some lunch; the leftover meat loaf I was gonna bring is still sitting on my kitchen counter. I was rushing around so much this morning I totally forgot it. Guess I've got the Monday brain."

"Please, it's no problem. I needed to get out of the office myself."

We proceeded to dig into our meals, not saying anything for a few minutes since we were both starving. Rashida hardly ever ate breakfast and all I'd had that morning was some coffee and a couple of plums.

"So you never told me what you ended up doing the other night," Rashida eventually noted, polishing off her chicken sandwich and wiping her mouth with a napkin. "I hope you didn't spend Friday night cuddling with your remote instead of with Kingston."

"For your information, I *did* spend Friday night with Kingston."

"Thank god. Did y'all finally do the do?"

"How does your mind automatically go to that?"

"What else is it supposed to go to?"

"We did not have sex, fast ass. But there *was*..."

Rashida looked up at me curiously. "There was what?"

I fiddled with the edge of my sandwich wrapper, debating whether or not I should tell Rashida about the argument Kingston and I had. When I looked back on it, part of me felt kind of silly. But the other part remained stubbornly justified in the suspicions I had.

"There was a little drama. I'd barely classify it as drama, really...more like a c-movie drama-lette..."

"What did you do, Adele?"

"I'm gonna go ahead and skip over my hurt that you automatically assume it was caused by me and just go ahead and tell you what happened. Even though I'm sure I'll regret it in a minute..."

I told Rashida about the minor tiff Kingston and I had; my accusations about why he was really interested in me, being forced to introduce him to Christopher before I was ready thanks to some damn busted pipes, Kingston's assurances that his interest in me was genuine and only about me, and us cuddling and kissing all night on the couch like some randy adolescents.

Rashida was actually frowning at me. "So..."

"Here we go..."

"You actually accused that man of having a Freudian complex? Just because he was missing her oxtail?"

"Yeah, that statement isn't Freudian at all," I muttered. "And that wasn't the *only* reason I jumped to that conclusion."

"Adele, even if he *is* attracted to you because you remind him of his mama, why is that so terrible? It's actually pretty common. And if he thinks highly of her, it should be considered a compliment."

"Well, clearly I didn't take it like that."

"Then you tried to put him out without letting him explain?"

"Figured all he was gonna do was deny it. Which would've only pissed me off more. And if I'm honest, I didn't trust myself not to fall for whatever he would've said. Which I kinda ended up doing, anyway."

"You know what that was, right? That insecurity was flaring up and you were looking for an excuse to push him away. And I'm glad he stood his ground until you listened to him."

"Rashida, I *melted* when he told me how he feels about me," I admitted, lowering my voice and glancing around to make sure no one heard me say that. "It was like I *felt* every word he was saying. No man's words have ever hit me like that. Even now, that freaks me out."

"Why?"

"Because I like him way too much! The first man that has made me yearn and daydream since Nate died is someone twelve years younger than me and *way* out of my league. I just keep expecting someone to come out of the bushes with the hidden cameras and reveal it was all some kind of dare or bet or challenge."

"I hate that you don't think any more of yourself than that."

"I think highly of myself, Rashida. But-"

"Don't say that when you're sitting up here talking about Kingston is '*way* out of your league'. And why? Because he's fine as hell? There are chiseled bodies all over this city; that's not anything unique."

I sighed. "Even so-"

"And I wish you would quit focusing on how old he is; he's a grown man. I'm sure he works, right? Has his own place and everything?"

"Yes, he works. Yes, he has his own place. He's a high school teacher."

"Even more reason to like him 'cause I sure as hell couldn't do that. Anyway, I'm glad that you ultimately admitted your feelings to him after all that mess you started but I have a feeling something like this is gonna come up again, when you'll listen to that little voice in your head and try to pump the brakes."

I wish I could've refuted that but she was probably right.

"I'm scared, Rashida," I admitted, slumping a little on the bench. My hands slid mindlessly along my thighs. "After so many letdowns, it's just hard to get my hopes up. But I want to, because I'm as into Kingston as he says he's into me. It just...it's freaking me out."

"Aww sweetie..." Rashida shot me an empathetic gaze. "Believe it or not, I get it. But if you want to be in a relationship, with Kingston or whoever else, you're just gonna have to step out on faith. Unfortunately there aren't any guarantees with this stuff; you just have to trust your instincts. And if you think Kingston is for real and worth the risk, just jump in and enjoy it."

She made it sound so easy. "What if it doesn't work out, though?"

"Then you'll deal with it," Rashida replied easily. "You're strong enough to do that. A man shouldn't make *or* break you, girl...they only have the power you let them have. You've got a good man who is into you, and the feeling is mutual; that's a great thing. *Let it be* a great thing."

That conversation stayed on my mind the rest of the day.

AFTER WORK AND A HALF-assed workout at the gym, I headed home with a tired body and churning thoughts. I felt mentally spent. Rashida's advice about Kingston replayed through my mind over and over. I knew she was right, about how I needed to stop trying to find what was wrong with my relationship with Kingston and just enjoy how right it felt. It was just my natural instinct to try to cushion a fall, even when I wasn't sure a fall was going to happen.

Christopher was in the kitchen when I entered the house, and when I heard him talking I figured he was on the phone. I started to call out and let him know I was there but when I heard the topic of discussion was his girlfriend Zuri, I decided to do a little eavesdropping.

"Yeah, we're still together," he confirmed to whoever he was talking to. Probably Dylan. "She was talking about doing something for our two month anniversary. I thought it was a little corny but it's a big deal to her, so..."

Two month anniversary? Yeah, kinda corny but sweet, if you chose to look at it like that.

"I'm here by myself," Christopher continued. Pause. "Man, you tryin' to get my head knocked off? No *way* I'm doing that. Mama would kill me if I tried to sneak Zuri over here while she was gone."

Damn right.

It made me feel good to hear my son doing the right thing even when he didn't think I was listening or watching. He was sixteen and I didn't expect him to be perfect, and I knew how strong peer pressure could be. Hearing him refuse to break my rule about having his girlfriend over unsupervised gave me a little relief.

After another minute or so of being nosey, I went on into the kitchen, making myself seen. Christopher was sitting at the kitchen island eating a huge bowl of strawberry ice cream. Lucky bastard.

He looked up and smiled when he saw me come in, putting down his spoon. "Hey, Ma."

"Hey baby."

"I'll call you back, man," he said into the phone. He moved to hang up then paused. "I don't know; sometime later." He ended the call and put the phone on the counter.

"Sometime later, what?" I asked him, eying his ice cream. He had crushed Oreos on top of it. "That was Dylan?"

"Yes, ma'am. He wanted to know when I'd be getting on the video game."

"Well, that homework better be done before you do. Speaking of that, where's that progress report you were supposed to get today?"

"I already put it on your bed."

"Good." I went over and gave him a hug, then shook my head at the container of my forgotten lunch still on the counter from that morning. "Boy, you didn't see this here? How come you didn't put it back in the refrigerator?"

"I figured you left it there on purpose."

"Why would I leave a container of leftovers out on purpose? Clearly I forgot it earlier."

Christopher just shrugged and shoved more ice cream into his mouth. Lord.

Shaking my head, I dumped the contents of the container into the trash before opening the fridge to see what I'd make for dinner. I really wasn't in the mood to cook anything and immediately began an internal debate of pizza or Chinese.

"Oh yeah, Ma, before I forget...since you still need to meet Zuri, how 'bout the four of us have dinner over here?"

"The four of us?"

"Me and Zuri, you and Kingston."

I closed the refrigerator. "I'm surprised you'd wanna do something like that."

"Well it was mostly Zuri's idea. But I figured it would be cool, too."

"Why do you say that?" I couldn't resist asking.

"Because Kingston seems all right. And this is the first boyfriend you've had since Dad died."

"Are you sure you're okay with that, baby?" I moved to join him at the island, leaning on my forearms across from him. "Me...being in a relationship?"

He shrugged. "Why wouldn't I be?"

"Because it's one thing for me to date but another for me to bring someone here and actually claim him. And I realize I never asked how you *really* felt about me and Kingston being together."

"Doesn't bother me. It's not like Dad *just* died; it's been years. I don't expect you to wanna be by yourself forever."

I peered at him over my glasses. "You're *sure*? It's okay if you feel some kinda way about it."

"Ma, I'm fine," he insisted, grabbing his empty bowl and moving towards the sink without looking at me. He sounded kinda testy to me, but I figured it was because I was still pestering him for a response when he had already given one. I don't know what it was I wanted him to say.

"All right, then," I conceded, letting it go. "I'll ask Kingston about the dinner but I can't imagine him having a problem with that."

"Good. I'll let Zuri know; can't wait for you to meet her, Ma. She's way better than any of the other girls I messed with. You're gonna love her."

"I'm sure I will," I made myself say.

"I'm gonna go finish my homework. What's for dinner?"

"Whatever I feel like ordering."

"I vote for pizza."

"Noted."

He sauntered out of the room and I adjusted my glasses, a concerned frown deepening as soon as I was alone. There was a bad feeling in my gut but I wasn't sure where it was coming from, or why. It bothered me as I went about changing out of my work clothes and throwing a load of laundry in the washing machine.

I was shuffling through the takeout menus when Kingston called.

"Hey, babe."

"Hey."

"What's wrong?"

"You don't miss much, do you?" I gave a half-hearted chuckle. "I said one word and you can tell something is wrong?"

"It's all in your tone. Got something on your mind? Another tough day at work?"

"No, work was fine." I went to my room and closed the door, then into my en suite, closing that door, as well. I knew I was going to be talking about Christopher and wanted to cover myself in case he decided to eavesdrop on me like I'd done on him earlier. "Something else is bugging me."

"What's up?"

"I'm a little concerned about Christopher. This girlfriend of his...I'm wondering about the influence she has on him."

"Did he do something?"

"No. At least, nothing that I know of. But he talks about this girl more than he's talked about anybody else. And I just have a strange feeling about all of it."

"Hmm."

"And it's not like I can punish him for something that hasn't happened. I've already asked all the gently-probing questions I can think of without making myself sound too paranoid. I don't know what it is but I just have a bad feeling."

"Is it possible that you just don't like that another female is taking a lot of the attention that Christopher used to give to you? He's growing up, babe."

"I...I wanna deny that but I guess I can't. Ugh, look, I don't have a problem with him having a girlfriend. Well, not enough to forbid it, anyway. I know Christopher is getting older and has his own interests that don't always include me. But this isn't just jealousy; call it mother's intuition."

"You might have me on the mother's intuition but I *do* work around kids Christopher's age every day, not to mention being a son to a single mother, myself. And one thing I hear kids complain about and that I dealt with when I was his age, is parents seeing a bunch of stuff in the news or wherever and then projecting that paranoia to their kids. And I get wanting to be cautious, but a lot of times what ends up happening is that you drive them to do the very thing you don't want them to do."

"Really?"

"Babe, I see it all the time. Dealt with it, myself. My mama swore up and down I was smoking cigarettes when I wasn't even thinking about that shit. Bugged me about it so much that after a while, I figured I might as well see what all the hype was about. Especially since she was so convinced I was already doing it, anyway. At least then I wouldn't be getting hounded for nothing."

"Wow." I bit my lip as I took in what he was saying. "That's something to think about."

"I don't have any kids so I'm certainly not trying to tell you what to do," Kingston insisted. "Just trying to give you something to think about, that's all. Keep your eyes open but don't stress yourself out if he hasn't even done anything wrong."

"I appreciate that, Kingston. It's hitting me that I'm venturing into territory I'm not quite prepared for; Christopher...doing his own thing. And his dad isn't here anymore to help me with that part."

"*I'm* here," Kingston assured, his voice wrapping around me like a hug. "Whatever you need, even if it's just a male point of view, just say the word. I know I can't take the place of his dad and I wouldn't even try to, but I'm more than willing to be there for you with Christopher however you need."

I couldn't hold back my grin if I tried. It was a really sweet thing for him to say, and I'd be lying if I said I didn't appreciate the hell out of it. Even if I didn't go running to Kingston for every little thing as far as Christopher was concerned, it was nice to know he was willing to listen and help should I need him to.

"Thank you for that," I told him, still cheesing. "It means a lot to me."

"My pleasure."

"Oh, um, Christopher suggested us having dinner with him and his girlfriend. Would you be okay with that?"

"No doubt. When?"

"Not sure yet; he just suggested it a little while ago. Apparently it was *her* idea. I'll let you know; it'll just be here at the house."

"Sounds like a plan. And I hope that whenever it is, you'll be nice to the girl."

My jaw dropped. "I'm never *not* nice to the lil' heffahs he brings over here."

"Adele."

"That was a joke, Kingston, come on. Of course I'll be nice to her. I'm sure there has to be a reason Christopher's nose is so open. I'm looking forward to seeing what it is."

"And *I'm* looking forward to watching you do that. It'll be better than anything on TV that night."

Chapter 11

DON'T TELL ME MOTHER'S intuition isn't a thing.

It had been a little over a week since Christopher suggested having our dates over for dinner and since then, he seemed different. He was on his phone twice as much as before, always wanted to stay after school for some reason or another, and when he *was* home, he stayed in his room. Usually he'd hang out in the kitchen with me while I made dinner or we'd watch a game or movie together some nights, but none of that was happening. All of a sudden, he just didn't seem interested in being around me.

"What's up with you, boy?" I asked when he started to retreat back to his room after dinner one night. "You know you're supposed to clean up this kitchen right after dinner."

"Can I do it later?" he whined, his shoulders slumping. "There's something I need to do first."

"*What* do you need to do first?"

Hesitating, he sucked his teeth. He *actually* sucked his teeth at me. "Can I just please be excused? I'll do the dishes before I go to bed."

Telling myself not to go off, I took a deep breath. "Is there something on your mind, baby? You've been in a mood for days. Is there anything going on I need to know about?"

"No."

Rearing, I blinked hard, looking at him like he'd lost his mind. "Uh, *no*? Did you forget your home training just like that?"

"No ma'am." His eyes were averted and he fidgeted impatiently. "Can I go?"

"Unless you can give me a legitimate reason why you need to, no you may not. This isn't anything new, Christopher; when we finish eating, you do the dishes. It's been like that since you could reach the sink."

He sucked his teeth again, a slight frown marring his brow. I had to give myself another minute because this attitude was ticking me off.

"Uh, unless you have some chicken stuck somewhere in your molars, I suggest you cut out the teeth sucking," I warned. "I don't know what's up with you lately, Christopher, but you *better* check your attitude. 'Cause you don't want me to get one back. I *promise* I'm better at it than you. And you won't like what comes of mine."

He glared at me and I glared right back. But after a few moments, his expression smoothed out and he started to look like his usual easygoing self. My frown remained, though. I wasn't falling for it.

"Sorry, Ma," he finally conceded. "I'll get the kitchen done now."

He proceeded to clear the dishes from the table, and I just sat there and eyed him, slightly thrown by the one-eighty change in demeanor but still miffed we'd had that little exchange at all. When he put in his earbuds so he could listen to music while he worked, I went into the living room, even more sure that I had reason to be concerned. Christopher wasn't flawless, but getting attitudes for no reason wasn't one of his trademarks. I could only attribute the recent change in his behavior to his little girlfriend Zuri, and I can't say it endeared me any to her.

I did call both Dad and Kingston to get their perspectives on it, though, since I had certainly never been a teenage boy and I wanted to be sure I wasn't being irrational. They both pretty much told me the same thing; these were just growing pains and it wasn't anything to be overly concerned about, as long as I kept my eyes open. I could only hope they were right about that.

IT WAS FINALLY TIME for this dinner. With Christopher going through his little phase and my trying not to stress over it (and not always succeeding), I didn't think it was going to happen. Meeting his girlfriend certainly wasn't at the forefront of my mind; really, with the hot-and-cold attitude roller coaster he was on lately, he was lucky his behind wasn't on punishment.

"I need a favor, Ma," Christopher announced, coming into the living room as I was straightening up the couch pillows. He had put on some kind of cologne, I noticed.

"What?"

"Can you not embarrass me tonight?"

Pausing, I slowly stood up straight and glared at him. "Excuse me?"

"I'm just saying...please don't say anything that'll embarrass me. You know how you get."

Reeling as I frowned so hard that it actually kinda hurt, I dropped the pillow in my hand and folded my arms. "And *how* is that?"

"You can be kinda sarcastic at times. I'm used to it but Zuri might take it some kinda way. I'm just asking you to be nice."

Ooh, the strength it took to hold my tongue at that. Reminding myself that he was probably extra nervous and paranoid because he was into this Zuri girl more than he'd been into anyone else, I took a deep breath and made myself not take any of this personally.

"Yeah, sure," I muttered, resuming my pillow-straightening. "When is she getting here? Dinner is just about ready."

"She just texted me that they'll be here in about fifteen minutes. Her dad is dropping her off. You can meet him, too."

"Great."

"Where is Kingston?"

"On his way."

"Is he gonna be late? That won't be a good look."

"Chill out, Christopher. It's just a dinner at the house, not Buckingham Palace."

"Zuri trips about folks being late to stuff. It's one of her pet peeves. Do you think I have time to change clothes?"

"You've changed clothes three times already, son. You look fine."

"Just *fine*?"

"Why are you acting like this is some kind of blind date? You've been with Zuri for almost three months now. You see her damn near every day at school. I'm sure most of your phone activity is devoted to her. I'm not sure what all this nervousness is for."

"I just don't want anything to go wrong. What is it you're making, again?"

Good grief. "Salmon, herbed potatoes, asparagus. Rolls."

"Hmm."

"What?"

"I'm trying to remember if Zuri likes asparagus or not..."

"Well, it's made now. So her highness is just gonna have to deal with it, regardless."

"You're being sarcastic, Ma."

"I'm getting it out of my system."

Cutting his eyes at me then looking down at the floor, he groaned in frustration. "We should've vacuumed in here. Are we using the good plates?"

I sighed, letting my head fall back.

"Crap, she'll be here in a minute..." He glanced at the time on his phone. "I'm gonna go change my shoes." And with that, he shot up the stairs.

Glad to have a break from his over-anxious ass, I went to take the rolls out of the oven. I was putting them in the seldom-used bread basket I'd gotten as a housewarming gift when I heard the doorbell ring. I figured Christopher was probably still doing his last-minute preening, so I went to answer the door.

"Hey, babe," Kingston greeted me, stepping into the house.

"Hey there, handsome," I smiled, accepting his peck on the lips before closing the door behind him. "Glad you could make it."

"Woman, please. I feel kinda honored that you're even willing to have me over like this; as your man and everything, doing the official first meetup with your son's girl."

"I hadn't thought about it like that but, true."

"Where's Christopher?"

"Probably changing into yet another outfit. Or putting on more cologne or doing some pushups or trying to grow a beard. He's been a nervous wreck all day."

Chuckling, Kingston removed his jacket. "He must be really into this girl, then. He cares what she thinks."

"Oh, he cares, all right. Between analyzing my menu and critiquing the housework, he actually asked me not to embarrass him."

"I hope you didn't take that personally."

"Tried not to."

"Just know it's more about him wanting to impress his girl than it is about anything being wrong with you. Y'all could be living in a mansion with servants and dope everything and he'd still be stressing."

"Mildly encouraging." I took his jacket and hung it in the side closet. "I just hope she's not one of those stuck-up demanding lil' heffahs with sky-high standards that Christopher thinks he needs to live up to."

"I'm willing to bet it's more about him just liking her a lot. Now give me a *real* kiss before he comes down here."

Automatically smiling, I didn't even bother fronting like I didn't want that. I just went into his arms and treated myself to those lips that I couldn't seem to get enough of.

"Hey, there's something I want to talk to you about before the night is over with," Kingston informed me in a low voice when the kiss tapered off. His face was still close to mine.

My smile faded a tiny bit. "What is it?"

Just then, Christopher bounded down the stairs. I instinctively started to back away from Kingston, but he wasn't trying to let go of me. And seeing us hugged up didn't seem to faze Christopher in the slightest, anyway.

"Hey, Kingston!" he greeted (with *way* more enthusiasm than I was expecting, I'll admit). "When did you get here?"

"Just a couple of minutes ago," Kingston replied, keeping one arm around my waist and using the other to slap hands with Christopher. "How's everything been going, man?"

"Fine. I'll be glad when school lets out for the summer, though."

"Yeah? What are you gonna have going on this summer?"

"There's a basketball camp I'm looking forward to. And Ma might let me go on a trip with my friend Dylan and his dad."

"Sounds like you've got a fun time lined up. I used to have to spend my summers working, mostly."

"Thankfully Ma won't let me get a job yet."

Since the two of them had practically forgotten about me anyway, I eased into the kitchen to finish prettying up the table for dinner. My mind was on whatever it was Kingston wanted to talk to me about later. I had no way of knowing if it was something good or bad, and that made my own anxiousness shoot through the roof. It tempted me to go tell Christopher that I didn't think Zuri would like his outfit so he'd go change again and Kingston could go ahead and tell me whatever it was he needed to tell me, because I already knew it was going to be on my mind all damn night.

When I heard the doorbell, I glanced at my watch and made my way back to the living room. Little miss stickler-for-time was a few minutes late.

"Ma, this is Zuri," Christopher introduced, shooting me an anxious glance before smiling at the girl now standing next to him. She was tall and nice enough-looking, but not someone I would have guessed Christopher would've been so flipped out over. I guess he didn't have a set type.

Plastering a smile on my face, I extended my hand. "Nice to meet you, Zuri, finally. I've certainly heard enough about you to feel like I kinda know you already."

"I'm glad we could finally meet, too. I've been telling Christopher we needed to make this happen for a while," Zuri replied, glancing at Christopher in what looked like an admonishing manner. I could see Kingston eyeing me.

"I thought I was going to get to meet your dad."

"Oh, he had to go; got an important phone call from work. But he said he looks forward to meeting you soon."

"Oh okay. Well, we're glad to have you. You met Kingston already?"

"I did, yes," Zuri confirmed with a blushing glance at Kingston. Geesh, he even had the teenagers swooning over him.

"Good. Well, we can go ahead and eat. Hope you're hungry."

"Starved. Thank you for having me over, Adele."

I blinked. Did this child just call me Adele??

"Uh, Zuri," Christopher jumped in before I could go off. "Just call her Ms. Mozley. She doesn't like for my friends to be so...casual like that."

"Really? Y'all do that here?"

Kingston had moved over to me and slyly grabbed my hand, stroking the underside of my wrist with his thumb. I usually would have enjoyed that affection but now it was doing nothing to soothe my ire. I officially didn't like this girl and I wanted her out of my house.

"Yes, we do that here," I informed her in a clipped tone. "If by *that* you mean teenagers respecting their elders."

Christopher was silently pleading with me to chill out but that was out the window. It was one thing to keep an open mind but quite another to be disrespected.

"Oh, I didn't mean anything by that," Zuri insisted. "It's just that we're not so formal in my house, that's all. My parents have always let me call them by their first names. It's more freeing, they said. Not so stiff and archaic."

"How progressive. But in *this* house, it doesn't go like that. So you can call me *Ms.* Adele. Call it a compromise."

"Sounds good," Zuri agreed, as if she had a choice. "And I see we already have something in common."

"Oh we do? What?"

"We both have a thing for younger men."

"What the f-"

"Whew! Uh, babe, let's go ahead and start dishing the food out while Christopher shows Zuri where she can wash her hands, huh?" Kingston quickly spoke up, turning and pulling me towards the kitchen. "My stomach is growling already, it smells so good."

I let him pull me away, which was probably a good thing because cussing my son's girlfriend out before we'd even had the bread would put a real damper on the rest of the evening.

"Babe, you have got to chill *out*," Kingston hissed at me once we were in the kitchen. He rubbed my arms. "This evening is gonna fall apart before it even starts if you tear her a new one."

"You heard what that lil' heffah said to me??"

"Yes, I did, and I'm not saying she wasn't out of line. But she clearly grew up in a different kind of household."

"No kidding."

"And you know your son better than I do but I'm sure he wouldn't be with her if she was a bad person."

I sighed. "I guess not."

"Right, so just calm down, take whatever she says with a grain of salt, and try to enjoy the evening, all right?" He kissed my forehead before pulling me in for a quick hug, which did help put me a little more at ease. "Try to think positively, babe."

"Yeah, I'll try. But she's already used up her free show-your-ass pass, so I hope it's out of her system. She doesn't get any more."

Kingston shook his head but he couldn't resist smiling. "Just remember who's the adult and who's the child, here."

"Tell *her* that. *I* already know."

Christopher and Zuri filed into the kitchen a few moments later, and I told myself to calm down and give the girl the benefit of the doubt. It could be possible she was nervous about meeting me. Sometimes people said stupid things when they were nervous. I certainly had.

As the meal kicked off, though, it became harder to hang on to the sliver of positive attitude I'd managed to scrape up. Zuri seemed to have an opinion on every damn thing and it was making me itch to sit and tolerate it.

"This salmon is good, Ms. Adele," she commented, even though I noticed she'd only taken one tiny bite of it. "I'm so glad you didn't make tilapia. You know that's a fake fish, right?"

"Fake but delicious."

She paused, her eyes wide. "Is that a joke?"

"Sure."

"Oh, good." She actually looked relieved. "I was going to pull up the article I wrote about that, if you weren't. It almost won an award. But there's no need for that now, since you already know. Unless you still wanna see it?"

"I'm good."

"So you're a writer, huh?" Kingston jumped in, looking at Zuri with a forced smile. "Is that what you want to do after graduation?"

"Oh no. I like writing but I want to do something that's gonna make money; I'm not trying to be broke. I *did* think about a career in journalism, though. Being the one delivering the news on TV every night would be a cool career, I think."

"Sure, yeah. That's admirable."

"Are these rolls gluten-free?" Zuri asked, pointing to the one perched on the edge of her plate.

"No, they're not," I quickly replied, taking a huge bite out of mine.

"That's too bad. They smell really good but I've been trying to stay away from the gluten."

"More for us," I shrugged. "Bread never lasts long around here, anyway, as much as Christopher loves it."

Clearing his throat, Christopher sat up a little straighter in his seat. "Um, actually, Ma, I'm going to step off the bread a little, too. Zuri said I'll feel a whole lot better if I start doing that."

"I wasn't aware you had an issue in the first place."

"It's just something I'm trying. Figured it couldn't hurt."

"So you're not eating bread now. That's what you're trying to tell me?"

"Just the bad kind of bread."

"Yeah, he doesn't need to be eating that stuff," Zuri stated. My face tightened. "I'm just glad he's finally listening to me about it."

"She said I should cut back on dairy, too," Christopher added. "We can help each other with that one, Ma."

"Oh, you don't eat dairy, either, Ms. Adele?" Zuri piped up with a smile. "Good for you!"

It was taking *all* of my effort, it really was. "I'm lactose intolerant," I muttered.

"Ouch. But at least there are all kinds of non-dairy alternatives to things now. So you're really not missing anything."

"I don't believe in fake dairy. But I've learned to live with it by now."

"Christopher, your elbow is on the table again," Zuri scolded through tight lips, giving him a look.

"My bad," Christopher quickly righted himself.

I opened my mouth to comment on that but I felt Kingston's hand grip my thigh under the table. Ooh, how I wanted this evening to be over.

After another half hour of Zuri, Kingston, and Christopher carrying on a conversation about whatever (I had to make myself tune them out in case the little girl said something to tick me off again; I just kept my ears open for my name), Christopher and Zuri cleared the dishes while I grabbed Kingston's hand and stalked upstairs to my room.

"Wow, I'm glad I finally get to come in here but I wish it was for another reason than you being pissed off and wanting to get away from somebody," Kingston joked, glancing around my room. Even though we'd been dating a while and he'd spent plenty of time at the house by then, we'd never been to my room. It was already hard enough fighting the temptation to jump his bones when we were on the living room couch. Me in a room with his sexy ass and a bed? "You know I can take your mind off all that, since we're in here."

I whipped around to face him. "Are you serious with that?"

"Not sure where *your* mind is but I was talking about tickling you."

"Don't you dare."

"Have you calmed down yet?"

"Not enough to go back down there."

"I get that she has strong opinions and a lot to say-"

"A *lot* to say."

"But that doesn't make her a bad person, Adele. And Christopher isn't complaining about it."

"Yeah, I see, which makes me wonder what she's done to my boy. Because Christopher can be described as a lot of things but *meek* is nowhere in there."

"I'm sure you know that having a crush on somebody can make you act differently, at least at first. I could tell you all kinds of stories about the stupid shit I did for girls back in the day." Kingston took my arm and gently pulled me to sit on the bed next to him. My mind was so consumed with my distaste for the girl down in the kitchen with my son that it didn't even register to me that I was actually in my bedroom with this ridiculously sexy man. "Haven't you ever done something foolish for a dude you were into?"

"No comment."

"That's what I thought. Give it some time, babe. This infatuation fog will clear after a while and Christopher will get to the real about how he feels about Zuri and the stuff she says and does. It might change things and it might not. But he has to realize it for himself."

"Ugh. Whatever. I know *I* don't like her, though. There's certainly no fog clouding *my* judgment."

"Yes, there is. It's just a different kind."

"Hmph." If this was who Christopher was into and they both respected my rules, I guess I'd just have to live with it. He was only sixteen; it's not like they were getting married. It actually made me miss the clingy motormouth Deena he'd brought over before. She wouldn't shut up but she was a sweetheart.

"Babe, since we're alone, remember when I said there was something I wanted to talk to you about?"

I'd temporarily forgotten about that but now that he reminded me, I felt my nerves wake up again.

"Yeah..."

Kingston shifted nervously. "Let me ask you...have you been seeing anybody else?"

"What?" He caught me off guard with that one. "No!"

"Really?"

"Why are you asking?" I frowned suspiciously. "Have *you*?"

"No, and I'm glad you haven't been, either. Because I want it to be just you and me."

Once his words registered, my frown melted and my jaw dropped slightly. "Wh-what?"

"I know we haven't really talked about this yet; I knew you were hesitant and I didn't want to push you about putting a label on us. It's kinda just been understood that we're together. But I still wanna put it out there. I've been thinking about it a lot the past couple of weeks, and I know I'm not trying to share you, Adele. I want to be the only man in your life. You're damn sure the only woman in mine."

"So you're saying you want us to be exclusive?" I felt the need to verify, even though what he said was pretty clear.

"Yeah. I want us to officially commit to each other. Put it out there that it's just the two of us in this. 'Cause I don't want anybody else. Are you good with that?"

I let out a breath, smiling in relief and excitement. My hand flew to my chest, feeling my thumping heart. Just like that, the name Zuri didn't even exist.

"I'm absolutely good with that," I responded, biting my lip.

He returned my smile, his fingers stroking the underside of my chin. "You thought it was going to be some kind of bad news, didn't you?"

"I don't know what you're talking about."

"Uh-huh. Well I hope I've put your mind at ease, about the situation downstairs *and* about us. I plan on going the distance with you, woman. And I'll tell you something else."

I just looked into his dark eyes, not trusting myself to speak.

"I'm falling for you," he informed, his voice dropping. "Hard. And I don't want you to feel compelled to say it back until you're ready to. I just hope when you are, you'll let me know."

His lips were on mine before I could respond. Which was a good thing because I had no words right then. My heart felt like I was falling for Kingston, too, but my head warned me to be cautious. To be *sure* that it wasn't just flattery and infatuation fueling whatever feelings were flooding my body right then.

For the moment, though, I just let Kingston ease on top of me on my bed and kiss me until my lips went numb.

Chapter 12

TRUE TO FORM, I REPLAYED Kingston's words in my mind over and over days after he said them.

He was falling for me, he said. Hard. This beautiful man that had taken over my heart and mind in the short time we'd been dating only wanted to be with *me*. It blew my mind.

I had just gotten to where I accepted that his interest and feelings for me were plausible. But now he was talking about *going the distance*, like he wanted us to be together long-term. I hadn't allowed my mind to go there but now that the thought was in my head...I didn't hate it.

What the *hell* was I doing??

I didn't want to agonize over this but it was pretty hard to put it out of my mind. Worrying about Christopher and his annoying girlfriend helped some. I didn't like the influence she seemed to have over him. But at the same time, I had to (repeatedly) remind myself that my opinion of her was just that; *my* opinion. I couldn't choose Christopher's girlfriends for him, no matter how much easier that would've made life for me.

"You must finally be getting some."

My head snapped to Ms. Corine, who was peering at me as I straightened up the items on her dresser. I had wandered in to see her that following Monday, mind still all over the place, and hadn't even noticed that I really hadn't said much since entering her room.

"What??"

"You've been preoccupied ever since you came in here. Plus you got a glow you don't usually have. So either you done finally opened that goody drawer back up or you pregnant."

I couldn't help but laugh. Lawd, Ms. Corine.

"Pregnancy ain't happening, Ms. Corine. And my *goody drawer* is still closed." *For the time being, at least.*

"Uh-huh."

"I *am* into someone, though," I admitted, perching myself on the edge of the dresser. "It's getting kinda deep."

"About damn time. Is it the same young man you talked about before or you done met somebody else?"

"*That* you remember, huh? Nope, same one. This kind of lightning only strikes once."

"Let me guess; you done fell for him but you fightin' it."

"Close...I feel like I'm *about* to fall for him but something about it makes me itch. For whatever reason, I just cannot make myself feel totally comfortable with all this. Every time I get past one hangup, I get stuck on another."

She peered at me for a few moments before motioning to the folding chair next to her. "Sit down right there."

I did what I was told and prepared myself for anything.

"I was married to my Charles for over thirty years before he died," she began. "He was my first love, father of my kids, blah blah blah."

"You've mentioned that."

"Yeah but what I haven't said nothin' about is the man I had *after* him."

My eyebrows shot up. "Oh?"

"Not a whole lot of folks knew about it 'cause at the time, I was a little embarrassed."

"Embarrassed? Why?"

"Charles had only been gone about a year when I met this man. I felt like it was too soon to be interested in anybody else but I couldn't get him out of my head. So I joined him for a show one night. After that, we kicked off a relationship that I enjoyed, but always felt a little guilty about."

"I can understand that. It makes sense that you were worried about upsetting your kids."

"I didn't give a damn about that. My kids were grown and off doing their own thing. What I was stuck on was if I was disrespecting my marriage to Charles by jumping into something else so soon after his passing. And if I'm honest, I wondered how it made me look."

"How did you get past that?"

"Never really did. I stayed with the man for a while, but my back-and-forth emotions about it ended up making him lose his patience. He ended it and to this day, I haven't fully gotten over it. Probably never will."

"Wow, Ms. Corine." I eyed her as she fiddled with the buttons on the TV remote in her lap. "Did you ever consider going back to him and trying again?"

"Thought about it. But by the time I worked up the nerve, he had met somebody else. Then he had to go and marry her. They're still together. Damn it."

"How do you know?"

"Turns out his daughter-in-law works here, at the front desk. I happened to see a family picture when I was going by there one day. Go figure. Small world, they say."

"Are you serious?"

"Couldn't make this up if I wanted to."

She could and we both knew it. Part of me wondered if this story was another concoction of her imagination but the bigger part was more focused on the overall message. If I didn't get myself together, I could lose Kingston. Even though he had insisted that he wasn't going anywhere and wouldn't let my issues drive him away, a person could only take so much.

I might not have been sure of a lot, but I was sure I didn't want Kingston to go anywhere.

When Rashida came over to the house later - and of course the subject of Kingston came up - I told her about Ms. Corine's story and how it made me think about my relationship.

"So you think Kingston might lose patience with your foot-dragging and move on to somebody else?" she asked me, kicking her heels off and curling her feet underneath her on the couch.

"It's not impossible."

"I thought you finally believed that Kingston's interest in you was genuine. What is it that has you hesitating now?"

"I wish I knew. And the fact that I *don't* know for sure is incredibly frustrating."

"Do you think you're disrespecting Nate's memory or the marriage you had with him somehow?"

"No, that's not it. If this was just a year or so after his death, that might've been it. But enough time has passed now, I believe. And before Nate passed, he made me promise to try to find someone else if anything ever happened to him."

"Adele, girl...I believe Kingston is here for as long as you'll let him be here. But I guess it's not impossible that he would run out of steam if you keep putting up a new obstacle every time he manages to knock one down. It's like you're blocking yourself from being truly happy with him."

I chewed my lip. "Can't say you're wrong about that."

"This is something you're going to have to figure out. I'd hate to see you end up like Ms. Corine, living with regret because you let your issues drive away a good man. *Especially* if they drive him into the arms of another woman."

That actually made me wince a little bit. The thought of Kingston with another woman made my chest hurt. I didn't want him with anyone but me.

So what the hell was my problem?

I liked him; he liked me. It shouldn't be this difficult. At this point in my life, I should have a better handle on this kind of stuff. I was in my damn forties, for pete's sake.

"Where's my godbaby?" Rashida asked, interrupting my mental self-kicking.

"Basketball game."

"How come you didn't go?"

"Where they're playing is almost an hour away. By the time I got off work and got out there, it would've been half over with. I was gonna try to get off early but he sent me a text this afternoon saying he didn't want me to worry about it."

"I thought he liked having you at his games."

"Once upon a time, yeah. But I guess that's just yet another thing that's changed about Christopher lately."

"And you still think it's because of his girlfriend?"

"Maybe not *all* because of her but I definitely feel she has a hand in it. There's something about her I don't like or trust."

"She's a year older than he is, right?"

"Yeah. And that made her feel we have 'something in common.'"

Rashida giggled. "I still can't believe she actually said you both like younger men. Though, technically, she's not wrong."

"Please." I rolled my eyes. "That coincidence hardly makes us BFFs. Kingston is definitely an anomaly."

"Another reason I like him for you. You needed to get out of your comfort zone."

"His age doesn't bother me anymore. But I know I need to figure out what *does*." My phone chimed and I grabbed it from the coffee table. I sucked my teeth when I saw the notification.

"What's wrong?" Rashida asked. "And do you have any wine?"

"Sure wish I did now. I think I see the reason Christopher didn't want me to come to his game." I held up my phone to show the picture he had been tagged in on Instagram. Of course by Zuri, who was there and proudly shouting him out.

"Ahh, he's got his girl there," Rashida observed, peering at the picture. "Well, hey. Maybe he didn't want you to go since he knows you don't like her."

"So what? I know how to act. And it's not like I have to sit with the girl. We can both be in the same gym."

"He doesn't want any drama. And it's not like that dinner you all had went that well, from what you told me."

"That wasn't *my* fault."

"You're the adult."

"I was nice to her, Rashida. She's the one who came in my house calling me by my first name and spouting her opinions nobody asked for. It's not like I put her out like I started to. She can thank Kingston for that one."

"Well, obviously Christopher really likes her, and apparently it's mutual. So you're going to have to find some way to deal with her."

"Hmph. I can't say I'm thrilled with the thought of him choosing her over me, though."

"Don't take it like that. You know he loves you. He's just growing up. And part of that is him not needing you as much anymore. That doesn't have to be a bad thing; you raised him right. Just trust that."

"You certainly have a lot of parental wisdom for someone who doesn't have any kids."

"I watch a lot of TV."

My phone chimed again, this time with a text from Kingston letting me know he wanted to see me. I smiled like the almost-in-love woman I was.

"That must be from Kingston," Rashida guessed with a smirk. "If a simple text has you blushing like that, I can just imagine how you're gonna be when you finally sleep with him."

"Does it always go back to sex with you?"

"Most of the time."

"We're waiting on that."

"Why? You saving it for marriage?"

"Please."

"I've never known you to have one of those stupid three or six-month rules."

"I don't have that. Though there's nothing wrong with them."

"I just feel like if two consenting adults want it and are on the same page, there's no use in waiting just to make yourself feel more conventional. Especially at our age. I'm too grown to be concerned about anyone's timetable other than my own."

"That rhymed."

"You can try to deflect all you want to. But I *know* you want a taste of that man. Especially since you haven't had any non-battery-operated action since Destiny's Child was a quartet."

"It has not been *that* damn long."

"Long enough, though."

I shook my head but Rashida wasn't totally off. I damn sure wanted Kingston. There had been *many* a night when I laid in bed and fantasized about him being in there with me. Similar fantasies in the shower, too.

After Rashida left, I wandered up to my room even though I needed to be getting dinner started. I stripped down and did something I didn't allow myself to do: look at myself fully naked in the mirror. It actually took a few moments for me to turn my eyes to my reflection, and when I did, I had to make myself not look away. My body was soft and plush, which would be good if I were a couch but not so ideal when it came to appealing to a stud muffin like Kingston.

I shoved that thought out of my head, though. Kingston had made it more than clear that he was attracted to me as is, and I wanted to believe that wouldn't change once he saw me undressed. I didn't bother with stuff like body shapers or waist trainers so he knew I wasn't chiseled, as much as he was always feeling on me. And when I considered that I ate what I wanted and usually just went through the motions with my workouts, my body could've looked a lot worse.

The good stuff: my DD breasts weren't exactly standing at attention but they still looked damn good, I thought.

My stomach wasn't flat (and never had been) but there were no rolls. It might've jiggled but it didn't hang. There was still a little cinch in my waist, amazingly.

I liked my innie belly button.

My hips were good and rounded, and my butt was a little dimply but abundant (two things I admittedly hated back in the day). And if thick thighs were still in, I was golden. Even if they were sprinkled with cellulite.

Thanks to brown sugar body scrubs and cocoa butter, my skin was soft and smooth. And deliciously scented.

Cute toes.

Yeah, I had a little more fat in some areas and jiggle in others that I didn't love. But I didn't look terrible; far from it. It was actually a relief to realize that; I'd had it set in my mind that my body was atrocious even though I hadn't allowed myself to *really* look at it in years. I felt the confidence shoot up my spine and make me stand up a little straighter.

"I'll be damned."

A COUPLE OF DAYS LATER, I headed up to Christopher's room when I got home from work. Since the day of the basketball game he absolved me of going to, he had spent most of the time in his room, when he was home. Conversation between us had grown stilted and minimal, and I was determined to get things back on track between us. Even if it meant agreeing to make more of an effort to get along with his girlfriend.

I did my usual knock before trying to open the door, but to my surprise, it was locked. He knew that was a no-no in my house.

"Christopher!" I yelled (because I was angry and because he was playing music). I banged on the door with the side of my fist. "Christopher, open this door!"

The music turned down slightly and I heard him moving around in there. I leaned in closer to see if I could hear him talking to anyone, but I couldn't.

A few moments later, he eased the door open. Barely.

Ignoring his *why are you bothering me* look, I stormed past him into the room, forcing the door open and making him stumble backwards a few steps. Looking around before turning my glare on him, I put a hand on my hip.

"Why are you in here with the door locked? You know good and well that's not allowed."

He shrugged. "I figured that rule didn't apply anymore since I'm almost seventeen."

"You were wrong."

"Come on, Ma. I should be able to have some privacy by now. What if you come in here while I'm changing clothes or something?"

"You don't have anything I haven't seen already. And privacy is for owners. *You* don't own anything. Everything you have up in here, you have because of *me*."

"Ma..."

"And you shouldn't be doing anything in here that you want me locked out of seeing."

"It's not like I'm doing drugs or building bombs or stuff like that. What's the big deal?"

"Don't lock this door anymore. Now that we've re-established that, I was going to ask if you wanted to go to a movie tonight."

"I can't." He plopped onto his bed.

I silently told myself not to get upset. "And why not?"

"You said Zuri could come over, remember?"

Damn, I'd forgotten about that. He had asked me that a couple days earlier.

"Oh yeah," I muttered. I glanced at my watch. "What time is she supposed to be getting here?"

"In about an hour. I was trying to clean my room before she got here."

"Don't know why that matters. It's not like she's gonna see it."

"She saw it when we were Facetiming. She said it's juvenile to have clothes all over the floor."

I both loved and didn't love that. I hated Christopher leaving clothes all over his bedroom floor, too. But apparently it didn't matter what *I* thought. Zuri calling it juvenile apparently made it an urgent issue, though.

"Yeah, well. Fine." I turned to leave the room, brushing my locs from my face. "Oh yeah, did you finish that research paper that's due Friday?"

"Almost."

"You need any help?"

"I've got it under control."

"If you say so. The grade on this one better be higher than the last one you did." I headed for the door.

"What's for dinner?"

"Chinese."

"Zuri doesn't like Chinese. Can we get something Italian?"

I was glad my back was turned because I had to squeeze my eyes shut and count to ten to stop myself from proclaiming just how little of a damn I gave about what Zuri liked.

But in my effort to be nice, I made myself say, through gritted teeth, "Sure."

By the time Zuri arrived, we had an assortment of Italian dishes and Christopher, freshly groomed, was all smiles. Of course he was happy now.

"This lasagna is really good," Zuri commented, helping herself to another serving.

I cut my eyes at her as I twirled spaghetti around my fork. "I'm surprised you like it so much, given your distaste for dairy and all."

"Oh, I'm not worried about that today," she dismissed with a wave of her hand. "I'm not in the mood."

Not in the mood? So she was flaky, too. Wonderful.

"I see."

"Ma, you like Zuri's hair?" Christopher asked me, looking a little eager. "She just got it done yesterday."

"It's nice," I replied, barely glancing at it.

"Thanks!" Zuri exclaimed, oblivious to my disinterest. "I figured I'd try these faux locs on for size; my friends and I have been thinking about starting locs for a while but haven't had the nerve to do it."

"It's not a big deal. If you change your mind, you can always comb them out. It's not like getting a tattoo."

"Oh, I have one of those already." She stood and lifted the back of her baby tee, revealing her name tattooed on her lower back in swirly letters. My jaw dropped.

"That's *hot*," Christopher observed with an appreciative grin. My head snapped to him but he was too busy ogling his girlfriend's tramp stamp.

"You should get one too, Adele, if you don't have one already," Zuri suggested, sitting back down. "I bet your boyfriend would like it, too. You're not too old."

My fork clanked to my plate. "Zuri, I'm gonna tell you this *one* more time. I want you to be comfortable here but you're gonna do that while respecting me and my house. It's Ms. Adele or Ms. Mozley. Your choice. But you do *not* address me like I'm one of your friends."

I could see Christopher's face turning red from the corner of my eye but I didn't care. I had already warned this little girl about this once.

"I'm sorry," Zuri murmured, shrinking in her seat a little bit. "It just slipped out. We're just a lot more free in our house. It won't happen again."

"You forgive her, right, Ma?" Christopher pointedly asked.

"Yeah, sure. All is forgiven." I chose to ignore that little comment about freedom and dropped my napkin onto my empty plate before standing. "I'm done. And I've got two huge baskets of laundry upstairs that needs my attention."

"We're going to do some homework down here."

"After we clean this stuff up," Zuri chimed in.

"All right." I turned and peered at them. "I'm sure I don't have to tell y'all to behave."

"Ma!"

"Hush, boy. I've been your age before so I know how it can go. Just a reminder; don't try to do anything while I'm upstairs that you wouldn't do while I'm downstairs."

"No problem, Ms. Adele. You don't have to worry about anything like that," Zuri assured me. "We're just going to be going over Christopher's research paper."

I glanced at Christopher, who averted his eyes.

Without another word, I went upstairs. For the most part, that visit had gone pretty well. I didn't have the overwhelming urge to put Zuri out like I did the first time she came over. That was progress, as far as I was concerned.

While I went about the task of folding laundry, I called to check on Dad and listen to him gripe about the latest women who tried to worm their way into his house and heart, then Rashida called to dish about some work drama and the trip she and her man Jared were getting ready to take. Then Kingston called.

"Hey, babe. What are you up to over there?"

"Oh, big fun over here. Folding laundry."

"I need to be doing that, myself. One of my least favorite chores, I admit."

"Something else we have in common."

"I love it. Hey, you have plans on Saturday night?"

"No, why?"

"I wanted to take you out. Go have a really nice dinner and then come back here to my place and...spend some time together."

My hands slowed in folding the shirt I was holding. There was no need acting like I didn't know what *spend some time together* meant.

"Oh..."

"What do you think about that? I know we usually hang out at your spot but I really want some uninterrupted time with you. Would Christopher be all right there by himself for an evening? Or could you make other arrangements for him?"

"Um, sure, yeah. I could always take him to Dad's, if I needed to. But he should be fine by himself for one night."

"So...is that a yes? To our night together?"

I knew any yes I gave would be to both the date and what would happen after. Rashida's words ran through my mind about waiting, or rather, how pointless waiting was if it was something I really wanted. And frankly, I was tired of denying myself.

"That's absolutely a yes," I replied with a smile.

"I can't wait."

Damn it, I couldn't either. Now I was going to be counting down to that night and over-analyzing everything up until the time he came to pick me up.

Kingston and I talked a few more minutes before he got a call from his mother and said he'd call me back. I was already giddy and looking forward to Saturday night, running through the things in my closet and wondering if I should make an emergency appointment with my loctician. As cheesy as it sounded, I wanted my first time with Kingston to be as perfect as I could make it.

Preoccupied, I headed downstairs to get some juice. I entered the living room and almost tripped over my own feet when I saw Christopher and Zuri making out on the couch.

Chapter 13

I WISHED I WAS THE kind of person that could immediately forget about stuff that bothered them.

Like when I slipped on an old burrito in the middle of the cafeteria back in high school and busted my ass in front of everybody. Or when I caught my college boyfriend cheating on me with my lab partner. When I went to kiss someone on a date and they pumped the brakes on me.

Or when I catch my son slobbing his girlfriend down on my couch.

I told myself it was no big deal. They were just kissing. No clothes had been removed. One of them wasn't on top of the other. Hands were where I could see them. And it was pretty funny how they jumped apart when they realized I was in the room.

As awkward as that scene was (and the days following between me and Christopher), I forced myself to put it out of my mind. I felt a lot better about it after I freaked out to Rashida for a while. And anyway, I had other things to focus on, like my date with Kingston.

Saturday night came quickly. I was still a bundle of nerves, but they were the good kind. Spending the night with Kingston was something I wanted and had thought about more times than I could count.

Of course I mentioned to Rashida that I was going out with Kingston, but as far as she knew, it was just a regular date. I didn't want to tell her about the intended first-time sex because she'd make a huge deal out of it, wanting to come over and choose everything I put on down to my underwear. I wouldn't put it past her to try to make me cram the Kama Sutra or do a bunch of stretching exercises beforehand. I didn't need any added pressure.

I turned on some Maxwell while I got dressed. Fresh locs, dewy complexion from an impulsive mini-facial, a dress that I dug from the crevices of my closet that was *way* shorter than I remembered, and a pair of platform heels that looked hotter than they felt completed my sex-expectant date night look.

"Oh my god, I look like a stripper who doesn't know they're past their prime," I muttered when I looked at myself in the full-length mirror, tugging on the dress. My head said to change into something more 'me' but the wannabe-thot-for-a-night self overruled that.

"Is that what you're wearing?"

I paused from trying to pin up my locs with my elbows resting on the vanity and my head ducked (because that's about as high as I could lift my arms) and turned to Christopher hovering in my bedroom doorway, looking at me strangely.

"What's wrong with it?" I knew what was wrong with it.

His eyes traveled down to my teal bodycon dress. "I, um...that doesn't look like something you usually wear."

"Well, yeah, but...just thought I'd try something different tonight, that's all."

"Did you borrow that from Auntie Rashida or something?"

"As if I could fit her clothes."

"That looks more like something she would wear."

True. "Ehh."

"Did you lose a bet?"

My arms dropped again. "Christopher, I do not look *that* bad."

"Not *bad*, just...not *you*."

He wasn't wrong. I didn't even feel like myself. But for whatever reason, I felt that doing something different was necessary, even though Kingston was plenty interested in the usual me.

And it would just figure that the most Christopher talked to me in days was about his distaste for my outfit.

I shooed him from my room before he could shame me anymore and finished getting ready. Kingston had texted that he was on his way and all that was on my mind was what he was going to think when he saw me. Would he think I looked ridiculous or appreciate the effort? Would he still want to sleep with me after seeing me in this? Was I about to blow it?

Losing my nerve, I hurried towards my closet to get the cute green maxi dress that I had designated as a backup. But before I could even get it off the hanger, I stopped myself.

This was a special night. Kingston was a special man. He deserved the *extra*.

I smeared my new lipstick over my lips with slightly shaky hands and added yet another layer of eyeliner, making sure I had the sexy smoky dramatic look I was going for. After some strategically-spritzed perfume, I made sure my purse was stocked with the essentials (mints, moist wipes, just-in-case condoms that I prayed he fit, lipstick, a compact, lotion, foldable ballet flats, spare set of panties) and grabbed my shoes, opting to wait until I got downstairs to put them on. No need in risking a twisted ankle before the evening even started.

I actually jumped when the doorbell finally rang. In a last-second impulsive decision, I decided to take my glasses off, placing them on a nearby end table. Taking a few deep breaths and whispering some encouraging words to myself, I checked the peephole before swinging open the door.

"Hey, sweetie!" I practically shouted, sounding as nervous as I felt.

Kingston smiled before his facial expression melted into something else as his eyes took note of my outfit. Then they wandered back up to my overdone makeup and hair that was already giving me a slight headache thanks to all the pins in it, holding my locs up in an updo I remembered seeing on YouTube once.

"Damn, babe..."

I shifted. "You mean that in the good way or the...*other* way?"

"You just..." His brows were still scrunched towards his sharp hairline as he gave me another perusal. "I surely wasn't expecting you to do it up like this."

Still not sure how to take that, I waved him inside, taking note of his gray blazer and dark slacks. "I just need another minute. And I can change, if necessary. I'm not sure where it is we're going but if this isn't appropriate-"

"No, it's not that," he insisted. He rubbed his chin. "You look fine for where we're going, if this is what you wanna wear. It's just a new look for you, that's all. At least, that *I've* seen."

Not having the nerve to dig into that statement, I scrunched my shoulders. "Just figured, why not? You know?"

"Sure, yeah." He peered at me. "Where are your glasses?"

"Decided to go without them this evening."

"You have contacts in?"

"Nope. I don't have any."

"How are you gonna see, Adele? You know you're near-sighted."

"I'll be all right."

He eyed me warily before shrugging, apparently figuring I knew what I was doing. Smiling, he reached for me. "Nice lipstick. Is it the kind that doesn't kiss off? If not, I hope you have some more."

I grinned, some of my tension easing a bit. "It's not supposed to kiss off but let's try it and see."

"Say less." He leaned in and kissed me, pulling me closer to him. His kiss felt like he was still attracted to me. I felt a teeny bit of my confidence return as I slid my arms around his neck. Or at least I started to. My damn dress was so tight I couldn't lift my arms high enough. So I just grabbed the sides of his blazer.

"I'll be right back," I murmured against his lips, stealing another peck.

Just then, we heard music blare from Christopher's room upstairs. It's crazy how I'd actually almost forgotten about him. I glanced up towards his room nervously.

"Everything okay?" Kingston asked, noticing my look.

"Not entirely..." I scratched the back of my head, digging a nail between my pinned locs. "Things with Christopher have been kind of off lately and I'm wondering if it's the best idea to leave him unsupervised like this. I probably should have had Rashida come over. Or taken him to Dad's."

"And you're just realizing this now?"

"I've admittedly been a bit preoccupied." I didn't want to admit all of the mental back-and-forth and almost crippling anxiety I'd experienced in the days leading up to this date. "And I didn't tell you but the other night, I caught him and his girlfriend going at it on my sofa."

Kingston's eyebrows shot up. "Whaaat? They were having sex down here??"

"What? No! They were kissing!"

"That's all?"

"That's *plenty*. I didn't go off on them or anything but I didn't leave them alone again, either. And things have been kinda strained between me and Christopher since."

"You want me to talk to him?"

"I-really?"

"Yeah, of course. If you wouldn't feel some kinda way about it."

"No, I wouldn't but...I'm just wondering how much he'd tell you, that's all."

"Only one way to find out. He might open up to me more than you think; there are some things a teenage boy doesn't want to discuss with his mama, no matter how close they are. Trust me."

I glanced at my watch, bringing it close to my face. "Do we have a reservation or something we're gonna miss?"

"We've got some time. Just say the word and I'll go up there. But know that if he tells me something in confidence, I won't break that. I want him to feel like he can trust me. But also know that I won't agree to keep anything from you that I feel you should absolutely know."

"Sounds fair. Okay, well, have at it. I'll wait."

"All right." He squeezed my hand before heading up the stairs.

Resisting the urge to go up myself and change outfits, I plopped onto the couch and grabbed my purse so I could refresh my lipstick. I heard Christopher's music fade, and listened for the sounds of Kingston coming back downstairs in defeat. But the minutes kept ticking by with him still up there, and my curiosity was driving me crazy.

I wanted to know what they were talking about. I knew Christopher liked Kingston, but I didn't think it was to the level where he would confide in him about stuff that he couldn't confide in me about. As much as I knew it made sense that he'd feel more comfortable talking to a man not terribly much older than him, it was still hard for me not to take that personally. I started to rub my eyes before I remembered I was wearing an insane amount of eyeliner.

"Babe."

My mind had been so all over the place that I hadn't even noticed Kingston had come back downstairs. Looking up, I cleared my throat and glanced at my watch again.

"Damn, did you two trade life stories?"

"It wasn't that long."

"Is everything okay? Should we just stay here and make it a Hulu-and-takeout night?"

He eyed me for a moment before shaking his head. "Not necessary, in my opinion. And that has nothing to do with my wanting to get you alone in my house. Christopher and I had a good talk about growing up and earning trust, and other stuff like that. He understands the responsibility that comes with staying here by himself all night."

"Hmm." I wasn't totally sold. While I believed Christopher might very well tell Kingston stuff he wouldn't tell me, I also believed he would say the right things so Kingston would give me a good enough report to get us out of the house.

"You ready?"

I blinked from my musings and realized Kingston was holding his hand out to me. Deciding that I wanted to go out with Kingston more than I wanted to give in to my mama paranoia, I placed my hand in his and let him pull me off the couch.

"Yep, let's go." I grabbed my things and moved towards the door, pausing in front of the stairs. "Christopher, we're leaving!"

I heard his door open. "Bye! Have fun!"

He certainly sounded like his old self all of a sudden. "I'll probably be back super late so don't try anything up in here."

"Don't worry, Ma. I'll be good."

"You better be. Love you."

"Love you, too. No dairy!"

"Humph."

My uneasiness about leaving Christopher alone eased only after I sent Rashida a quick text from Kingston's passenger seat (with the phone abnormally close to my face) asking her to do a random pop-in, and she agreed. I tried to chill out and focus on the night ahead with my man. It was going to be a beautiful evening.

Or it would've been had I not almost busted my ass walking into the fancy steakhouse Kingston had taken me to. Damn platform heels.

"Whoa!" Kingston reached out to grab my waist before I crashed to the ground. "Babe, you all right?"

"Ugh...yeah," I grunted, my face flaming. I kept my eyes away from Kingston's or anyone else's. "Guess I haven't broken these shoes in enough yet. And I didn't see that damn curb, there."

"Babe, put your glasses on."

"They're in the car. I'll be fine."

"You good to walk inside?"

Ignoring the slight pain in my ankle, I straightened and forced a smile. "Of course."

Once we were inside, I felt even sillier. My outfit was totally out of place compared to the other patrons and the man whose hand I was holding. Kingston had this sexy polished look going and there I was looking like the woman who paid for his company via some shady app. I kicked myself for the outfit choice while simultaneously trying to act like I was the hottest thing in the room.

"Hope you're hungry, babe," Kingston commented once we were seated and had placed our drink orders. He looked over the menu the server had just given him. "I heard this place has a ribeye worth dreaming about."

"Ooh, that sounds good." Then I remembered the body-hugging dress I was wearing and silently cursed myself again. I didn't want to gorge on steak and sides (and dessert) and then have to worry about holding in a post-meal pooch in this dress. But I also didn't believe in ordering salad on a date.

"I think I might go with something a little lighter, though," I mused, fighting to keep my face and voice neutral. I brought the menu closer to my face and made myself look away from the steak section. "Maybe something with grilled chicken..."

He looked up at me curiously. "I thought you loved steak. That's the main reason I chose this place."

"I do; I love it. And I can already see six things on here that I'd love to have a taste of."

"Well, get what you want. Don't try to be cute with it on my account. One of the things I love about you is how much you openly love food."

"Yeah?" My eyes drifted back to that steak section. "Most men don't see that as a redeeming quality."

"I'm not like most men. Haven't you figured that out by now?"

Smiling – because I couldn't help it – I winked at him. "Touché, Mr. Farrell."

The waiter reappeared with our drinks and then took our orders. I ordered the chicken. Then changed it to steak. Then changed it back to chicken. After a couple more times of this, both the waiter and Kingston were forcing patience and I knew it.

"I'm sorry," I expressed, feeling like an idiot. Why was I acting like this was my first date? "I'll take the New York strip with mushroom sauce and cheddar grits."

"And how would you like your steak prepared?"

"Medium well is good."

"Very good, ma'am." The waiter noted my selection on his pad and then turned to Kingston. "And for you, sir?"

"The twelve-ounce ribeye with blue cheese crumbles and pimento mac and cheese. Cooked medium, please."

Of course he was decisive. He had plenty of time to solidify his choice during all my flip-flopping.

After the waiter left, I felt Kingston's leg brush against mine under the table. I glanced at him, hating that the image wasn't as clear as it would've been if I had my glasses on. I wasn't even able to fully appreciate all the sexiness.

"You're flirting with me," I accused with a smile.

"Damn right."

"Don't be trying to get fresh in here."

"I'll save the bulk of it for when we get back to my spot. But in the meantime," he reached across the table for my hand. "I'm more than satisfied just appreciating the view from here."

My face and some other parts got warm at his compliment. I briefly ducked my head, grinning. "You're gonna make me have Mr. Waiter make our order to-go."

"Girl, don't play with me. We'll be on the first thing smokin' outta here."

"I guess we should control ourselves. Wouldn't want to deprive you of that delicious ribeye."

"Damn that. I'm *looking* at the main course I want."

Officially horny, I clenched my thighs together under the table and jutted my breasts forward a little. One good thing about that dress was how it showed off the girls.

"Oh yeah?"

"Yeah. And you're gonna make me dive across this table if you keep serving those up to me like that."

Giggling, I managed to forget about all of the awkwardness and embarrassment from earlier. I remembered why I was so into Kingston; our rapport, his attention to me, his knack for making me feel like the only woman in existence.

All of our playful sexual banter pushed what was going to happen later to the forefront of my mind, though. Before the night was over, this beautiful man was going to see me naked. The remembrance sent a little chill through me.

Then I warmed again when I realized I'd also be seeing *him* naked.

To say I was looking forward to that was a huge understatement. I'd gotten to feel Kingston's body through his clothes and had the pleasure of seeing him with his shirt off a few times (good *lawd*) but I hadn't seen the whole shebang.

But once I was done ogling and appreciating that body of his, at some point things would move to the bed. It had been a long time since I'd gotten any; not since Nate died six years earlier. I was never one to brag on my sexual skills but I liked to think I could hold my own. And I had to ignore that little voice popping up in the back of my mind reminding me that Kingston probably got a lot more action than I did.

The thought only reminded me that we needed to have a conversation before anything happened. I was far from a prude but I needed to know a little more about him before I let him inside my body.

"What's on your mind, babe?"

I blinked, catching myself before I rubbed my eyes again. This was exactly why I didn't usually wear a lot of makeup. Should've sprung for the smudge-proof stuff.

"A couple of things," I hedged, running a finger along his knuckles. I opened my mouth to ask about the sexual history stuff, but what came out was, "What else did you and Christopher talk about?"

He shrugged. "A few things. Some stuff about him and Zuri, a couple of things about school. And we had a talk about respect and attitude and how he should treat you."

"Hmm. What school stuff?"

"Just that he's still not sure about what he wants to do after high school, and that it embarrasses him when he talks about it with his friends, especially Zuri. Apparently she has her own ideas about what he should do."

"Hmph," I grunted. "I bet she does."

"They've butted heads about it. But I let him know that there was nothing wrong with being unsure about that; he has plenty of time to make that decision. And he shouldn't feel pressured into anything."

"Very true. So...the stuff about him and Zuri?"

"*That* I can't tell you, babe. It was some man-to-man stuff that he asked me to keep between us. But rest assured, it's nothing you should be too worried about. It's pretty typical stuff for boys his age."

If only that put my mind at ease. It didn't totally sit well with me that Kingston and Christopher shared information between them that they didn't want me to know.

"Hmm." I frowned briefly but quickly erased it. I refused to get upset. "Guess I gotta respect that. Thank you for talking to him."

"Thank me later." He winked at me.

I bit my lip as our food came. And I was so, so glad I didn't get that chicken.

Dinner was great, but my mind was already fast-forwarding to the latter part of the evening. And with the way Kingston kept looking at me from across the table, I could tell his was, too.

Finally, after desserts of apple pie for me and walnut baklava for him, we left and headed to his place. I managed to get to the car without further injuring or embarrassing myself, and checked my phone. Rashida had sent me a message letting me know all was well with Christopher, so I relaxed and tried to mentally prepare myself for what was coming.

"You gonna put your glasses on now?" Kingston asked me as he pulled out of the parking lot.

Even though I needed to stop being stupid and do it, I just shrugged and squinted at the blobs of light on the road in front of us. "I'm all right."

"Babe, what are you doing?"

"Not sure what you're talking about."

"Adele."

"Kingston."

He glanced over at me but didn't say anything else. We just rode in silence, listening to the light jazz on the radio and me trying to ignore that slight pain still in my ankle. *And* my toes. I swear I was going to burn those shoes.

We pulled up to his house and I felt the briefly-forgotten anxiety come back. While I had no doubts that I wanted to sleep with Kingston, I couldn't help but worry if my...*performance* would measure up to whatever standards he had.

Good god, this man is going to see me naked in a minute!

Stop it! I had to tell myself, again, to stop worrying and just go with the flow. I wouldn't be there if he didn't want me there.

Kingston came around to help me out of the car, which was good because my feet were pretty much numb by then. He held on to my hand as we headed into the house, one of us rather gingerly, and once inside, I couldn't even take time to appreciate how he'd rearranged his furniture since I was there last because I was too busy trying to get to the couch and off my feet.

"I have some wine, if you want some," Kingston offered, removing his blazer.

"Red or wh-ah, hell, it doesn't even matter. Sure."

After he got us both glasses of what I guessed to be some kind of merlot, he joined me on the couch and watched as I immediately gulped down half my glass.

"Are you ready to stop this now?"

I glanced at him curiously. "Why'd you offer me the wine if you don't want me to drink it?"

"I'm not talking about the wine, Adele. I'm talking about you feeling the need to change yourself to the point of discomfort when it's not necessary."

Discomfort? I'd passed that a couple of hours ago.

I started to continue the whole oblivious game but decided that I was tired of it. I sighed and set my glass down on the coffee table.

"I guess I had it in my head that I had to be a certain way for tonight."

"Why, though? What have I said or done to make you think you needed to change *anything* about yourself?"

"Nothing. I came up with this foolishness all on my own."

"So end the foolishness, babe. Take off those shoes that are obviously killing you. Put your glasses back on. Let your hair down. You don't have to torture yourself to make me desire you. I've wanted you since the beginning."

As soon as those shoes were off my feet, I felt a hundred times better. I let out a long sigh of relief as my head fell back momentarily. The back-to-Adele session continued when I slipped my glasses back on and hurriedly yanked out all the bobby pins holding up my locs. I had to yank my arms up just to be able to reach them all and heard the fabric of my dress rip, but I didn't care. I wouldn't be wearing this shit again.

Taking a few minutes to massage my sore scalp, I actually closed my eyes and moaned at how good it felt.

And apparently Kingston got a little jealous about that because while I was still massaging, he knelt in front of me, gently eased my legs open so he could position himself between them, and started kissing my neck. My arms fell around his shoulders as I leaned my head back farther so he could get deeper in there.

"You smell amazing," he whispered as he licked across my collarbone.

"You *feel* amazing," I breathed, biting my lip.

"I want you, Adele. I've always wanted you." He leaned up to kiss my lips, moaning as he did so. "You don't ever have to change anything about yourself for me. I'm perfectly happy with the original package. Okay?"

Hearing him say that made me kick myself for making such a fool out of myself all evening. I could have enjoyed the night a lot more if I had worn something more comfortable and not tried to look like some kind of sex kitten.

But instead of dwelling on it and bumming myself out, I just tucked it away for future reference and let Kingston resume our kiss, his arm sliding under my lower back as he shifted upwards, treating me to the feel of his bulge between my legs. I immediately shuddered, damn near having an orgasm right then.

He started to grind against me, and my legs lifted around his waist, hiking my short dress up even further. My nervousness melted with every stroke of Kingston's tongue against mine, and it fizzled into oblivion when I felt my nipples being teased through my dress. I gasped, digging my nails into his back through his shirt.

"You wanna go to the room?" he murmured, looking at me with half-lidded eyes that caused a whole new rush down below.

Good thing I brought that spare set of panties.

"Absolutely," I agreed, eager to get back to it.

He pushed himself up and then grabbed my hands, practically yanking me off the couch.

"Wow, you're even stronger than I thought," I observed appreciatively. "I didn't expect-*Kingston*!!"

He had actually hoisted me onto his shoulder and was carrying me to his bedroom, like it was nothing. I don't think a man had *ever* picked me up like that, and it sent my horniness into overdrive.

Once we were inside his bedroom, I half expected him to toss me onto the bed. But he set me down gently, giving me that look again that almost made me whimper out loud.

"Need me to help you out of that dress?" he asked, running his hands around my hips to my ass.

"How 'bout you go ahead and get out of that shirt and those pants while I go and freshen up a little bit?" I suggested, my hands already pulling his shirt from his waistband.

"Whatever you like."

"Would you happen to have a t-shirt I could put on?"

I saw a flash of confusion cross his face, but he just said, "Yeah, over here," as he went over to his walnut dresser and retrieved a large black t-shirt. Handing it to me, he nodded towards the en suite. "Take your time."

"I won't be long." I gave him a lingering kiss before turning and strutting towards the bathroom.

I just needed a minute, that's all. When Kingston was grinding on me on the couch I was close to losing it, and I knew if we went straight to the bed, I'd be shuddering and convulsing way sooner than I wanted to. And if history continued, that would be pretty much it for me; I was frustratingly one-and-done. I never could relate to the tales of people (including Rashida) who claimed to just keep going and going until their limbs gave out. After a good orgasm, all I usually wanted to do was go to sleep. And I wanted – needed - this first time with Kingston to last longer than a playlist song.

Taking a whole lot of deep breaths, I peeled out of the uncomfortable bodycon dress and slipped into Kingston's shirt, automatically feeling better. There was a spare washcloth and towel on the counter, and I grabbed the washcloth and some of his face wash to get my overdone makeup off my face. I looked in the medicine cabinet for the cocoa butter, smiling as I spread it over my face, remembering when he'd told me he'd gotten that and a few other items to keep there for me when I came over. Such a sweetheart. You'd think he'd given me the Hope Diamond, as touched and excited as I'd gotten about that.

Once done, I looked at myself in the wall-length mirror and felt worlds better. And I had calmed down enough to where I was sure I wouldn't explode the second Kingston put his lips back on me.

Kingston was on the other side of his bed when I emerged from the bathroom, in nothing but his black boxer briefs.

"*Damn*," I muttered before I could stop myself, my eyes tightening in appreciation.

He grinned. "Glad you like. You good?"

"Yeah. I'm great." I inched towards the bed.

"Babe, I can tell you're a little nervous. And I know you probably still have it in your head that I'm not going to like your body as much as I say I will."

I didn't want to admit that, so I just hunched my shoulders slightly and looked down at my red toenail polish.

"So I'm hoping this will put your mind at ease a little bit."

I looked up in time to see him turn his back to me and lower his briefs. My mouth fell open.

"What the *hell*..."

"It's burned," he explained, referencing the huge scar going across his butt. "I sat on a heater when I was a kid."

"And *why* would you-"

"My cousin bet me five bucks and two candy bars, so I did it. Didn't think it would be that bad through my underwear. But it was, and I couldn't get up quick enough. It used to look a lot worse than this but it's still pretty embarrassing."

"Wow..." I continued to look at his deformity, and even though it was somewhere that nobody would see unless he showed it to them, it somehow made me feel a lot better about my own insecurities.

Now he seemed a lot less like some intimidating image of perfection and more like a regular man.

Still an incredibly hot and sexy man, though.

He pulled his briefs back up and turned back around to face me.

"You wanna leave now?" he asked teasingly, although I could see a glimmer of nervousness in his eyes when he asked me that.

"Of course not," I quickly insisted, smiling at him. "If anything, this makes me feel closer to you."

"Yeah?"

"Yeah. Come over here."

He quickly rounded the bed and came into my arms, and I pulled his face to mine. We each sighed as he gathered me close to him, squeezing me so tight that I actually gasped. He buried his face in the crook of my neck.

"You make me so happy, Adele." It was a whisper but I heard it. And it turned me to mush.

"You make me happy, too."

He really did. In that moment, I couldn't imagine my life without Kingston in it.

Lifting his head, he bit his lip as he looked me up and down. "I'm about to make you a *lot* happier, baby."

With that, he grabbed the t-shirt and lifted it over my head before I had time to agonize over it. Not that I would have. I was feeling a lot more comfortable than when I got there so when he took my nakedness in with his eyes, drinking in every inch, I didn't feel the need to cover or suck in anything. And apparently, I didn't need to.

"So fucking sexy," he growled.

Emboldened, I stepped forward and yanked those briefs of his back down. And when I got a first close-up glimpse of that thirty-three year old dick, I actually licked my lips. It looked more delicious than that steak I had earlier.

"You've got condoms, right?" I verified, eyes still between his legs. I was so busy drooling over his dick that I temporarily forgot I'd brought some myself, just in case.

"More than enough." He began stroking himself, causing my jaw to drop slightly. After I groaned in appreciation and enjoyed the show for a moment, I boldly slid my hands between my own legs. My eyes closed as I shivered slightly, whimpering as a frown of pleasure furrowed my brow. My feet moved wider apart as I got more into it, almost forgetting that Kingston was standing right there.

When I finally opened my eyes, the dick-stroking had stopped and he was breathing heavily watching me, looking like he was about to explode.

This man is gonna tear me apart.

He yanked me to him and kissed me so hard that I actually thought I was going to fall over. He had a tight fistful of my locs as he turned and walked me backwards towards the bed. My hands clawed at him, sliding up and down his muscled back down to the scar on his ass, appreciating everything I touched.

As soon as I was on my back on the bed, he had my breast in his mouth and a hand between my legs. My back arched violently as I let out some kind of noise I didn't recognize. I hadn't had this in years and my body almost didn't know how to act. Kingston was going to make me lose my mind, I could already tell.

And when he slid down, threw my legs over his shoulders and lifted up to his knees so I was balancing on my own shoulders as he began tasting my wetness, I was sure I was getting ready to meet the Lord. Because the way he proceeded to eat my coochie had me wondering if my heart could take it.

"*Fuck*, Kingston!" I screamed, my hands yanking on the sheets.

That only fueled him to kick up the intensity. I swear I didn't think a human tongue could do what he was doing to me right then.

"I love how you're loving it," he whispered against my lower lips, making me shudder like I'd stuck my finger in a socket. "I've been *dreaming* about getting my hands on you like this, babe..."

"You and me both. Shit, just like that..." I gasped as he started some kind of tongue twirl-suck combo that had my eyes rolling back.

"Mmm-hmm," he moaned, continuing to torture me. "Tell me you like it."

"*Like* it?? Oh *baby*...let me put it like this; we're never breaking up."

"Oh I could've told you that."

I felt like I was getting close and part of me wanted to tell him to ease up, but the rest was having no parts of doing anything to stop the best fucking head I'd had in my life. I was no idiot.

Thankfully, Kingston must have sensed that I was getting close to the mountaintop because he began to taper off, sliding those lips to my inner thigh and gently sucking the sensitive skin there, though he couldn't resist still occasionally going back to the good stuff.

"There are so many things I wanna do to you, baby," he said in between licks, my writhing hips locked in his grip. He gave it one final tongue kiss-suck (*oh my god*) before gently lowering my legs, quickly crawling up and covering my body with his. He dove for my mouth, his fingers teasing my nipples as we shared an intense, sloppy, moan-filled kiss. "But I need to get inside you *now*. I *need* to get inside you; don't make me wait, baby, please..."

"Yes," I immediately breathed, fingertips digging into his back. I would've given him my kidney right then. "Yes, *now*, Kingston..."

After quickly grabbing a condom and covering himself, he wasted no time getting back in position, resuming our kiss as he brought his tip right to my opening. Another delicious shudder tore through my body.

"*Shiiiiit*," I whimpered as he slowly slid inside of me, my brows twisting in pleasure. I almost wanted to cry, it felt so damn good.

"*Damn*, baby," he concurred, shuddering as he pushed himself in further. "You feel amazing...I want you so fucking bad, Adele."

We were just building up steam when he looked at my face and gently reached for my glasses.

"*Now* you can take these off."

Chapter 14

MY DAD AND I WERE PRETTY close. Always were. But our relationship wasn't perfect by any means.

I had the fun of being an only child, and got a lot of attention from my parents growing up. My silly self thought it was because they just loved me a lot or something, but I accidentally learned there was more to it than that.

Before my mother Nettie died, I overheard her and my dad talking one night through their bedroom door. I was about seventeen and had just gotten home from softball practice (which I only played because my friends did; I barely got into any of the games); I was going back to let them know I was there, but stopped when I heard them talking and noticed that I was the topic of conversation:

"Stuart, you can't spend that money!" My mama had hissed. "That's for Adele's prom!"

"Ain't nobody even asked her yet," Dad countered. "I doubt she'll even be goin.'"

"She *wants* to go. You know that."

"So she's gonna go by herself? All her friends will be there with their boyfriends and you know she ain't had none of those. At least none that *I* know of."

"Doesn't mean she can't get one, Stuart."

"Nettie. I love my daughter; Lord knows I do. But she ain't what the boys go for. If she could get a boyfriend she'd have gotten one by now. She's eighteen."

"She's *seventeen*. But..." I heard my mama sigh. "I guess you have a point, as much as it kills me to admit it. *I* think she's beautiful but not everybody looks at her like I do. She doesn't fix herself up or anything, still has that baby fat, she refuses to let me relax her hair..."

"She ain't ugly," Dad insisted. "But...I can't call her beautiful, as much as I hate to say it. And the boys clearly can't, either."

I just stood there, too shocked to react. I didn't cry or let them know I was out there listening. All I did was go to my room.

In all the years since, Dad didn't know I heard him say that about me.

Whether or not I realized it, those words stuck in my head from then on. Even after I got older and started putting more care into my appearance (I was admittedly a tomboy when I was a teenager and didn't care for much of the girly stuff), I always thought there was only so much I'd be able to do.

Thankfully I had my wonderful sense of humor for men to focus on instead of my looks. But that only made them want to hang out with me, not fall in love with me.

Until Kingston, that is.

He hadn't confessed love for me yet, but I wouldn't be surprised if I heard the L-word sooner than later. He'd made it known several times that he was falling for me, and hard. And it was mutual, as much as that freaked me out.

And *speaking* of Kingston...

That man, that man.

Kingston was either going to be my fountain of youth or the death of me.

After the night I spent at his house, it was official; I craved him. I was hooked. He put it on me in the kind of way you read about but don't quite believe. *No* man had sexed me down like that, including my late husband, which I felt I should've been more ashamed than I was to admit.

And that one-and-done thing? Yeah, not an issue.

It was going to be hard to not fantasize about all of this while I was introducing Kingston to my dad. After Christopher had talked about Kingston so much while he was over there one day, Dad had started hinting that I bring Kingston over to meet him.

Well, 'hinting' isn't really the right word. In Dad's classic fashion, he told me to *bring his ass over there.*

"I wanna meet this man that has my grandson's ear so much," Dad told me. "And that you've been spending so much time with. Haven't met any of your man friends after Nate passed."

"Yeah, well, none of them really stuck around long enough to get to that part," I droned, wondering what I could say to get out of this but knowing there was nothing.

"Well, seems like this one is sticking around. You've certainly been in a better mood. And Christopher talks on and on about him. So I wanna meet the young man."

"Sure," I agreed, because I felt I had to.

Part of me hoped Kingston would have some kind of problem with meeting Dad but I knew better than that. He was totally on board.

"Hell yeah!" he enthusiastically agreed when I mentioned it to him over the phone one night.

"Why '*hell* yeah'? This isn't anything to get excited about, Kingston. *I'm* damn sure not."

"I think it is. You introducing me to your dad must mean you're pretty serious about me."

"I'm plenty serious about you, sweetie, but honestly, this is more because of his insistence than anything else."

"If you were dead-set against it, though, I'm sure it wouldn't happen. I mean, you *are* a grown woman."

"Yeah, I'm grown. But that's still my dad. And I'm not really in the mood to get cussed out."

"Well, whatever. I'm looking forward to it."

"Uh-huh. I'll go ahead and warn you; Dad can be kinda blunt. And gruff. Borderline insensitive sometimes. But he means well. Usually."

"I can handle that."

"He'll probably ask you a bunch of questions. Don't be surprised if our age difference becomes a topic of discussion."

"So like father, like daughter, huh?"

I paused. "That's real funny. If you've noticed, I stopped obsessing about that a while ago."

"True. And I'm proud of you for that. I'm glad you've finally relaxed about us, period. That paranoia you used to have is pretty much gone."

"Didn't wanna keep driving us both crazy. And you *did* give me some rather prime ding-a-ling on that date. And a couple of nights after that. And this morning."

He chuckled. "Believe me, I'm equally as satisfied. Do you know how hard it's been trying to focus in my classes when I keep fantasizing about your sexy ass all day? It was hard as hell leaving you this morning, but I wanted to be out before Christopher got up. You don't think he heard us, do you?"

"As loud as his music was? Doubtful. But Christopher's not an idiot; I'm sure he has an idea that we're doing grown folks things in my room. No need in trying to front about it."

"Well, I'm comfortable with it if you are. I was just glad you pulled me into your room in the first place 'cause I damn sure wanted to go. And where did you learn that thing you did with your tongue?"

I couldn't help but giggle. "This old dog knows a few tricks."

"Nothing old about you, babe. But keep bringing those kinds of tricks. I'm thrilled that you're such a freak in the sheets. Do you even *have* a gag reflex?"

Busting out laughing, I fell back onto the pillow on my bed, gently biting my nail between my teeth as I rolled over to my side. I felt like a giddy teenager.

Though, when I thought about it, I never had anybody to feel like this about when I was an *actual* teenager. Realizing that made me remember what Dad said about me back in the day.

But as I had done so many times over the years, I pushed it to the back of my mind.

So that weekend, I figured we might as well go ahead and get this little introduction over with. Kingston, Christopher, and I headed over to Dad's, with Christopher and I giving all the last-minute warnings we could think of.

"He'll probably think you're a pretty boy," Christopher told him from the backseat. "Well, he'll probably just say it."

"Wouldn't be the first time I've heard that," Kingston replied with a smile, winking at me.

"Try not to take it personal."

"I won't. And it's personal*ly*, man."

"Oh, yeah. Zuri's always correcting me on that one, too."

"Dad will probably ask you a bunch of personal questions," I chimed in, trying not to roll my eyes at the mention of Zuri's name. "He's not very censored. And he'll likely be drinking whiskey but don't expect him to offer you any."

Kingston chuckled. "Y'all, this isn't the first time I've met a girlfriend's father. I've been grilled every which way you can think of. I can handle it, believe me."

I liked his confidence. But my trepidation didn't budge.

And with good reason, since Dad started in on Kingston as soon as we walked through the door.

"You one of those metrosexuals?"

I put my head in my hands but Kingston only laughed.

"I like to take care of myself, yes sir. I don't do spa days, though. Kinda draw the line at that."

"Hmph," Dad grunted, openly giving Kingston the once-over. "I guess that's good. Well, come on in here and sit down."

I trudged behind the three main men in my life into Dad's living room, wondering how long we were going to be there.

"So," Dad began, swirling his tumbler of whiskey in his hand that hung over the arm of his recliner, "How old are you? I can tell you're way younger than Adele."

"Not *way* younger..." I muttered.

"I'm thirty-three, sir," Kingston answered good-naturedly.

"And you got a thing for older women?" Dad asked him.

"I have a thing for *Adele*," Kingston clarified, matching Dad's direct gaze. "Her age really doesn't mean anything to me."

Lord, he was making me blush in front of my dad. And my son. I both hated and loved it.

"Hmph. You been married before? You know she's a widow, right?"

"I do. But no sir, I haven't been married yet."

"You wanna marry Adele?"

"It's not a conversation she and I have had yet but I can't say it hasn't crossed my mind. But I know we're nowhere near that point yet, regardless."

Christopher glanced over at me as my eyebrows shot up in surprise. Kingston actually thought about marrying me?

"And Adele is the only woman you're datin', huh?"

"Yes, sir."

"Why? Young, strappin' man like yourself probably gets plenty of attention, I'd bet."

Kingston shrugged. "I get my share. But when you have the one you want, everybody else becomes irrelevant. And Adele is the only woman I want."

Dad stared hard at Kingston, then glanced at me. I couldn't help but smile at Kingston's words. Any other man, I'd be suspicious that they were just saying what they thought my dad wanted to hear. Hell, if this meeting was happening with Kingston a couple of months earlier, that's probably what I would've thought he was doing, too. But thankfully, I was past the point of doubting his sincerity.

"That sounds good," Dad grunted, and I steeled myself for whatever else was coming because I knew he wasn't going to leave it at that. "So you mean to tell me that...you can see yourself being satisfied with *Adele* for the long haul?"

Kingston's eyes flitted over to me and I felt my face tighten. It didn't take a genius to get what Dad was trying to say.

Why in the world would a man like Kingston want to spend his life with an old troll like me? Surely he could have any woman he wanted, right?

"Not a doubt in my mind, sir," Kingston insisted, his voice strong. "And I consider myself fortunate that she chose to accept me. Having her and Christopher in my life means a lot to me. I'm not going to do anything to mess that up."

"I see." Dad took a sip of his whiskey.

I pretty much tuned them out after that. As much as I wanted to make myself not care about it, Dad's words stung. Apparently even now, after all these years, he still didn't think I was pretty enough.

Before I totally lost my composure, I got up and went into the kitchen, mumbling something about getting some water. I took my time, grabbing a bottle out of the case that Dad never bothered putting in the refrigerator, and leaned against the counter. I tried to tell myself that what Dad said didn't matter; it was just his opinion. I liked myself, and Kingston was happy with how I was. That's all that mattered.

But I guess there was a part of me that still wanted my Dad's approval. To hear him call me beautiful or pretty or even cute just *once*.

Eventually Christopher came into the kitchen, looking at me with concern. "You all right, Ma?"

"Yeah. Yeah, I'm fine."

I heard loud banter and laughter from the living room. I guess Kingston had passed Dad's test and they were buddies now.

"Granddad finally stopped grilling Kingston," Christopher reported, glancing towards the living room. "They were starting to talk about the election. It kinda felt like school so I got outta there."

I gave a half-hearted chuckle and set the water bottle on the counter, looking at the fading wallpaper behind the stove.

Christopher came to stand next to me and stuck his hands in his pockets. "Ma, I wanted to tell you I was sorry."

I looked up at him. "For what?"

"For how I've been acting. I know it wasn't right. And Kingston told me I needed to check myself and apologize to you, but to make sure I meant it when I did."

"Really? He said that?"

"Yes, ma'am. He said that as much as you do for me, you're the *last* person I should be acting funny towards. And I know he's right."

"I appreciate you saying that, baby," I replied, gently rubbing his arm. "And I appreciate you listening to Kingston. It's nice that you can confide in him like that."

"Yeah. I love you but there's some stuff that I'm a little embarrassed to talk to you or Auntie Rashida about. And Granddad...I just don't think he'll *get* it sometimes, you know? Kingston is real easy and cool to talk to. I admitted that I felt some kinda way that you don't like Zuri."

"I know..."

"But he said that you not liking her doesn't mean I can start treating you differently."

"Well, yeah. Girls are gonna come and go but I'll always be your mother. And my concern for you is always first and foremost, so I hope you keep that in mind whenever I don't gush over your girlfriends. At the end of the day, it's just my opinion; you're getting to the age where I have to step back a little and trust you to make your own choices. Within reason, of course."

"I appreciate that, Ma. And I know Zuri can be a lot; she gets on *my* nerves sometimes, too. But I'm into her and she's into me. I like hanging out with her."

"And making out with her on my couch."

His face immediately flushed. "Ma!"

"Sorry, baby, I couldn't resist that one." I smiled at him. "And I get it. You like who you like."

"Like you and Kingston like each other."

Tucking some locs behind my ear, I cleared my throat and nodded, my smile widening automatically. "Yep. I like him a lot."

"Good." We heard another peal of laughter from the living room. "Seems like Granddad likes him, too."

"Hmm." I told myself to stop worrying about what Dad said. If I wasn't going to call him on it (and I wasn't) there was no sense in bumming myself out.

Christopher and I hung out in the kitchen for a little while longer until we heard the doorbell. I curiously looked in the direction of the front door.

"Who is that?" Christopher wondered.

"Who knows," I shrugged. "Probably another one of Dad's admirers."

"He has a girlfriend?"

"I don't know if they call it that at his age. But it doesn't matter, anyway; the only thing Dad really wants from these women is for them to leave him alone."

We headed back into the living room to see a copper-skinned older woman standing near Dad's chair, holding a canvas bag that I was sure contained some kind of hopefully-enticing goodies for Dad. I noted her sassy short gray haircut and nude pumps.

"You really didn't have to bring anything, Edna," Dad was telling her. "I told you I already have enough food to last me 'til the Lord comes."

"Yes, I remember you said that. That's why I figured I'd bring you some other things you might need for the house; towels, bed sheets, soaps, and some of that whiskey you're always drinking."

"That's really nice of you and all, but-"

"Well, hello," Edna greeted, noticing me and Christopher. She smiled pleasantly. "And you are?"

"I'm Adele, Stuart's daughter," I replied, going over to shake her hand. "And this is my son, Christopher."

"It's nice to meet the both of you." Edna eyed me as I moved to stand next to Kingston. "And this young man that answered the door...is this your brother? Cousin?"

Kingston's arm slid around my waist. "No, ma'am. I'm Kingston, Adele's man."

"Her-her *what*? You two are in a *relationship*?"

"Yes, we are," I replied before Kingston could, probably a little more defiantly than necessary. I lifted my chin, daring her to say something else.

"Well, I'll be..." Edna marveled, putting a hand on her hip. She eyed Kingston up and down. "And here I was about to suggest introducing you to my granddaughter. Just how old *are* you, young man?"

"You sure are asking a bunch of questions," Dad griped before either of us could reply.

"Well I'm sorry, I don't mean to be rude," Edna insisted to Dad before turning her attention back to Kingston. "You are *very* handsome. And I think it's a beautiful thing that you're the type of man who isn't all about looks in a woman and more about the content of her character. That's rare nowadays."

Well, damn. Just diss me right to my face.

"All right, time to go," Dad announced, moving towards the door. "Thanks for the towels but next time, call before you come over here."

"Just one second, Mr. Dobbs," Kingston spoke up, holding up a hand. He took a couple of steps forward, his frustrated scowl on full display. "With all due respect, ma'am, I don't appreciate you insulting my woman like that."

Edna gasped, her hand flying to her chest. Drama queen.

"Insult?? I wasn't trying to-"

"That was a clear dig at Adele that you just made, and you know it. And not that I care what you or anyone else thinks about it, but I have no problem letting it be known that I'm attracted to *everything* about Adele; from her looks to her personality to how good of a mother she is to everything else. And *nobody* is going to disrespect her in front of me."

Christopher nodded in agreement, coming over to put an encouraging arm around my shoulders. He looked like he wanted to speak up himself, but probably figured he couldn't get away with disrespecting an elder, even if it was in my defense. I gave him a grateful glance as I tried to decide just how much I wanted to go off on this bitch myself. On a scale of one to ten, I was hovering around an eighteen.

"I wasn't trying to be disrespectful; I apologize if it came across that way," Edna stated, her brown eyes moving to me. "I'm sure you're a lovely woman, Adele, and certainly attractive in your own way-"

"Nope, we're not doing that," Kingston interjected, shaking his head. "She's attractive in *every* way. *I'm* the lucky one. Maybe one day Mr. Dobbs or another gentleman will be as into you as I am into Adele, and you won't have to try so hard by bringing towels and alcohol and bed sheets you wish you could sleep with him on."

My jaw dropped as Edna gasped and Christopher tried not to laugh. Even Dad was smirking a little bit.

"Bye, Edna," he said to her, moving back towards his recliner.

Stunned, Edna glanced back towards me and Kingston before hurrying out of the house, taking her bribery gifts with her.

"I'm sorry if I was out of line, sir," Kingston said to Dad once the door slammed. "But I don't play when it comes to Adele and hearing what that woman said pissed me off."

"No problem here," Dad insisted with a wave of his hand. "I don't mind you puttin' her in her place. She needed it. And I like to know my daughter is with a man who is gonna stand up for her."

I didn't bother mentioning that it would have been nice if my *father* had stood up for me, too. But I guess he wouldn't since he probably shared Edna's opinion.

We left not too long after that. I wanted to get out of my dad's house.

There wasn't a whole lot of conversation in the car during the ride back to my place. Christopher was on his phone in the backseat, and Kingston seemed to sense that something was on my mind and was probably waiting until we were alone to ask me about it. He just drove, placing a hand on my leg as he did so.

Once we all got back to my house, I started to fix something for dinner but Kingston thankfully offered to just order something. I wasn't in the mood to cook or do much of anything else; I just plopped onto the couch as Christopher went up to his room, asking us to let him know when the food got there.

"What's wrong, babe?" Kingston asked, placing a warm hand on my thigh as he joined me on the couch.

I hunched a shoulder, not really wanting to talk about it. "It's nothing."

I could feel his eyes on me. "You sure about that? Or did what happened at your dad's bother you?"

Glancing at him, I took in his concerned expression. "Yeah, it did. Whether or not it should've, it did."

"Is it what the lady said, or what your dad said?"

"Neither felt great," I mumbled, looking away. "Though at least what Dad said wasn't anything new. He's never thought I was much to look at and apparently still doesn't."

"You care what he thinks that much?"

"It's not a good feeling knowing your own father doesn't think you're attractive enough to appeal to a handsome man. He never pulled this with Nate. But then again, Nate was my age and wasn't the obvious hunk you are."

He took my hand, but I kept my head turned away from him. "Do you believe what I said to them, when I said that I loved everything about you and that I consider myself the lucky one, or do you think I was just putting on?"

"I...I believe you. It's just..." I sighed, suddenly exhausted. Easing my hand from his, I swiped my fingertips under my glasses, catching the tears that were threatening to fall. "I don't expect you to get this, Kingston."

"Then help me understand, Adele. I want to."

"Let's not do this. It's *my* problem and I know you might sympathize, but you'll never really get it."

"Adele, please don't push me out," he pleaded, taking my hand again and trying to get me to look at him. "I'm the one on your side, remember? I'm gonna *always* have your back, babe. You don't have to worry about that."

Yeah, but for how long? How long will it be before you have to defend me so many times that you start wondering if there's a point to what everyone else thinks?

"I'm going to lie down," I announced, standing. His hand fell from mine. "I just need a minute."

"You want me to leave?"

Yes. No. Hell, I don't know what I want right now.

"You've gotta be here when the food is delivered, right?" I tried to sound lighthearted but didn't quite pull it off. Not trusting myself to say anything else, I just headed upstairs, praying Kingston didn't come up there trying to comfort me.

Chapter 15

"ADELE, WHAT ARE YOU doing?"

"Hmm?" I looked over at Rashida. "What? What do you mean?"

"You're putting yogurt in the mashed potatoes."

"Shit!" I glanced at the sour cream that I was *supposed* to use and sighed, grabbing the saucepan and stomping over to the trashcan. It only took a few seconds of scraping out the ruined potatoes that I lost energy for it all and just chucked the whole thing in.

"Adele..."

"I'm fine, Rashida," I snapped, grabbing a sponge and giving the counter a furious and needless scrubbing. I needed to keep myself occupied.

"You're *not*, and it's obvious. You've been acting funny for a few days now. Even Kingston called me, worried about you."

My eyes snapped to her. "He what??"

"He's concerned about you, Adele. Ever since that visit at your dad's, you've been distancing yourself from him, he said; barely taking his calls or responding to his messages, and he said he hasn't seen you since then, despite his efforts. He's worried you're working up the nerve to end things."

My hand that was scrubbing the counter slowed. "Did he tell you what happened?"

"Yeah, he mentioned what happened at your dad's, as far as Daddy Dobbs and that lady making their little comments.

Kingston also told me he checked them, too. Did he not do that?"

"Yes. He immediately came to my defense."

"So what's going on? Why are you punishing Kingston for something he didn't even do?"

"I'm not trying to punish anybody. But I *am* wondering if..."

She eyed me pointedly, a suspicious glint in her eye. "If...?"

"If this relationship is headed towards a dead end."

"Why would it be? Just because a couple of people have stupid opinions?"

"It's not just about that. No, I didn't love hearing that stuff but it's nothing I haven't heard before. I'm thinking about Kingston. Is he going to get tired of *having* to defend me and our relationship to people? Will he at some point start looking at me differently? We've only been together a few months; maybe the novelty will wear off for him."

"I thought you were finally at ease about you two. So *one* visit to your dad's changed all that?"

"I'm gonna tell you like I told Kingston; I don't expect you to get any of this. You *can't*. You've never been dismissed because of your outward appearance. You don't have a *clue* what it's like for *nothing* you do to yourself being good enough for most people."

"Adele-"

"And it's *so* easy for people to say 'don't worry about what other folks think', or 'as long as you love yourself that's all that should matter', and all that. I'm not even saying that stuff isn't true. But it's different when you're in it."

She just looked at me helplessly.

"And over the years I've managed to develop some kind of shield against that stuff," I continued. "But hearing your own *father* doubt you hits different, Rashida. It just does. And I'm sorry if it disappoints you to hear it but it hurts. I'm not a machine; I'm human and I feel shit. It *hurts*."

I was crying and didn't try to stop it. My emotions had been all over the place in the few days since the visit to Dad's, and I'd been trying to hold stuff in around Christopher because I didn't want him worrying about me. But he was off with his friend Dylan, and it felt good to release all of this, finally.

Rashida got up from the stool and quickly rounded the counter to give me a hug. Her warm hand pressed my head to her shoulder, and I let out the rest of the tears I'd been holding in.

"Adele," she soothed after a few moments of my sobbing, "Girl, I am so sorry. You're right; it *is* easy for me to tell you how you should feel or react to things. I shouldn't do that."

I just sniffed and nodded, head still on her shoulder.

"I'm just gonna ask you, though, to *please* not put Kingston in the category with those other people," she gently continued, rubbing my back. "That man is all in with you. He sounded genuinely worried when he called me; the thought of losing you scares him. And I *know* you have feelings for him, too."

I abruptly stood and moved over to snatch a paper towel from the roll, removing my glasses to wipe my eyes. "Yeah, I do. A lot."

"And you don't *really* want to end things with him, right?"

"No, Rashida, I don't. But I'd rather hurt now than way down the line when I'm head over heels in love with the man and Christopher has started looking at him as some kind of stepdad. Hell, he probably does that already."

"But that's a blessing, Adele, not something to run from. Kingston is everything you've said you wanted in a man. Don't throw him away just because you're having a moment."

"A *moment* would have been over with by now. I've been all over the place for days."

"Even so. Don't try to convince yourself that you can't have a happy ending with Kingston. 'Cause you'll be even more miserable if you let him go, whether you want to admit it or not."

She was right about that one.

"Try having some faith in him and your relationship. And if necessary, confront your dad. Let him know how what he said made you feel."

I almost laughed. "For what? It's not like he's gonna apologize."

"It's not about getting an apology from him, Adele. It's just about purging that hurt and frustration you've been holding onto for so long. Getting it off your chest. At least he'll know how you feel about it."

Maybe she had a point. But having a heart-to-heart with Stuart Dobbs wasn't something at the top of my wish list.

"I'll have to think about that one," I sniffed, cleaning my glasses with the edge of my shirt before returning them to my face.

"Good. And while you're thinking about that, please also reconsider ending things with Kingston. I'd just hate for you to do something you'd regret."

"MA, CAN I GO TO THE movies with Zuri?"

I was on my bed holding a book, but I couldn't have told you what it said if you paid me. My concentration was shot. "Huh?"

"I asked if I can go to the movies with Zuri."

"Oh." I sat up a little straighter, glancing at the book in my hands as if I didn't know how it got there. I plopped it down next to me on the bed and rubbed the back of my neck wearily. "Yeah, I guess. Just make sure you're back before curfew."

"I will. Are you gonna do something with Kingston?"

My chest burned upon hearing his name. We still hadn't really spoken; just exchanged some texts. "I don't know."

"You should. He's a good guy, Ma. I really like him."

Great. "I'm glad to hear that, baby."

"And it's really cool of him to let me call him when I need to."

My head snapped up. "What? You two call each other?"

"Yeah, he gave me his number a few weeks ago. I didn't think I'd use it but after me and Zuri had another fight, I wanted to get his advice. We've been calling or texting since then."

Well, this was news to me. I wonder why Kingston didn't mention that he'd given my son his number. What *else* didn't I know about?

After Christopher left, I felt my annoyance continue to multiply. I felt some kind of way about Kingston keeping this bit of information from me. My hand itched to call him and go off, but I knew that wouldn't have been the smartest thing to do. I was way too emotional.

I needed to get out of the house. If I continued to sit there, my imagination would just keep going off on its own.

In the next half hour, I was at the gym. And since I had all this frustration to work off, I was putting in actual effort while I huffed away on the elliptical or pushed weights on one of the Nautilus machines. Sweat poured down my face and stung my eyes, but I didn't bother using the towel that was slung over my shoulder.

I *really* missed Kingston. It was crazy that something as simple as taking my man to meet my dad caused such a turnaround in my outlook on our relationship. Kingston hadn't even been the one in the wrong, yet he was the one I was shutting out. Granted, I hadn't talked to Dad since that visit, either, but he and I only talked once or twice a week, anyway, tops. And since Dad loved to be left alone, he probably didn't even notice that I hadn't called him since I left from over there.

Now that working out was occupying most of my aggression, I could recognize that the fair thing to do would be to call Kingston. He deserved to at least know what was going on in my head, however I could manage to explain it.

And when it came down to it, I was too grown to be shutting my man out with no explanation.

After about an hour of an actual workout, I took a long turn at the water fountain (I'd been too frazzled when I left the house to bring my own bottle) and went to the locker room. My sweatshirt and headwrap were soaked, and my face flushed. I looked a mess but I strangely felt a little better. I'd go home, take a long hot shower, then try to figure out what I'd say to-

"Kingston *did* that, girl," I heard some woman say as they entered the locker room. She and another woman headed over to their lockers. I noticed she had a long ponytail and one of those cute matching workout sets you saw on social media ads. And her abs? The only way I'd be able to get those would be in a plastic surgeon's office. "I can't *wait* to see him again."

"So you two had a good time, huh?" her friend, equally as cute and fit, asked her with a knowing grin.

"You know it. I've had my eye on him for a long time and I finally got him to go out with me. And let me tell you; I won't have to worry about chasing him anymore. He already wants to hook up again."

"Kita, girl, I'm glad you finally snagged that. 'Cause I was getting a little tired of hearing you bitch about how he wouldn't give you any play."

"Yeah, well, that's all over with now. It's Kita and Kingston from here on out."

My hands were actually shaking. I couldn't believe my ears. So I fall back for a few days and he goes off and gets with somebody else without even letting me know??

And of course it had to be with someone who looked like some kind of cinnamon-skinned fitness model. He wouldn't have to worry about anybody questioning his reason for being with *her*, that was for damn sure.

Yanking my bag out of its locker, I stormed out of the gym, knowing I looked like some kind of madwoman but not caring. I didn't even want to go home first; my hands steered my car straight to Kingston's house, hoping he was home but knowing I'd just camp out in the driveway until he was, if not. Tears were stinging my eyes but I made myself blink them away. I didn't want him to see me crying over him.

I'd save that for when I got home later.

Thankfully, Kingston's car was there when I screeched up to his house. Before I could stop and tell myself to calm down, I was banging on his door, shifting my weight from side to side and breathing fire.

The door swung open and Kingston appeared with a frown. "Adele? What the hell is going on?"

I pushed past him into the house, not even bothering to get out of the foyer before I stopped and turned on him. "I get that I've been making myself scarce lately but I didn't expect you to move on already."

His frown deepened. "What are you talking about?"

"I'm talking about you and Kita, Kingston."

"Who?"

"*Kita*. I just heard her talking about you at the gym. Apparently she's been after you for a while now and I guess my acting like an asshole gave you a reason to finally indulge her."

He pushed the door closed and came to stand right in front of me. He already seemed as angry as I was. "So you mean to tell me that the first time I get to see or talk to you in days is because of you coming over here to accuse me of cheating on you?"

"I don't hear you denying it."

"I'm absolutely denying it. I haven't gotten with anybody else, Adele. I don't even know anybody named Kita. What, you think I'm the *only* person on this planet named Kingston??"

My mouth opened to say something else but nothing came out. It hadn't even occurred to me that the women could've been talking about somebody else.

So, I felt like an idiot. As hot with anger as I'd been moments before, now the coldness of shame was flooding over me so much I actually started to shiver a little bit. (It might've also been the fact that Kingston always kept his house on the cool side and I was standing there in sweaty clothes. But I'm sure it was mostly the shame thing).

Feeling the need to save face still, I jutted my chin and blurted, "Well, what about you giving Christopher your number and you two calling and texting without my knowing about it? Why didn't you tell me about *that*?"

He scoffed and shook his head. "I offered him that the night I went up and talked to him before you and I went to the steakhouse. Didn't even really expect him to use it. And honestly, I forgot about it until he hit me up a week or two ago. Are you trying to act like I somehow did you wrong with that, too?"

"I'm just saying, Kingston; Christopher is my son. That's something I should've known about."

"Okay, Adele, fine; if that's how you wanna play it, I apologize for *forgetting* to let you know I gave Christopher my number. You happy?"

I glared at him.

"Now," he crossed his arms over his chest. "Your turn."

I took a tiny step back. "What are you talking about?"

"Now *you* need to apologize to *me*."

"For?"

"Are you joking? Some people disrespect you, I have your back, yet you shut *me* out for days with nothing but a few high school texts to pacify me. And then you jet over here accusing me of some unjustified cheating bullshit, which is a *complete* slap in my face."

I sighed. "Okay, maybe how I came at you was jacked up but *surely* you can understand how I would make that mistake."

"No, I don't. Because I *thought* I was with a grown-ass woman, and a grown-ass woman would know better than to jump to conclusions based off some random conversation she overheard from a couple of strangers at the gym."

My face burned as I looked at the floor.

"More importantly, Adele, I thought we were beyond all this. I thought you believed me when I said that you had my heart and I don't want anybody else. Here, you want my phone?" He yanked it out of his pocket and held it out to me with an arched brow. "You can go through my contacts, my social media, all my messaging platforms, whatever you want. I'll give you all my passwords. You won't find a damn thing."

Even though a small part of me wanted to call his bluff, the bigger part of me believed him. And I felt stupid enough as it was.

"Kingston, I don't need to do all that. I just..."

"You just *what*, Adele? What is it? Are you trying to end things with me?"

"No! I just-I don't know! This is hard for me, Kingston! Can't you understand that?"

"Honestly no, I can't, because you won't talk to me! You just tell me I won't 'get it' and then shut me out when I'm trying to be here for you! You're not the only one that can get hurt, here, Adele; when you do that kind of shit, it hurts!" He slapped his chest, every impassioned word coming out of his mouth making me feel more and more like an asshole. "I've been patient, consistent, respectful of your boundaries, more than willing to win your trust, and nothing seems to be good enough. I mean, *damn*, what else do you want me to do to prove how much I'm in love with you??"

It took a few seconds for his words to register but when they did, my eyes slowly lifted back up to his face. He was angry but I still saw some tenderness in those eyes of his.

"You..." I cleared my throat, a hand gripping my damp shirt over my chest. "You what?"

"You heard me, babe. I'm in love with you. And I *know* you have feelings for me. So I don't know why you're so afraid of me and what we have. Why you keep trying to find reasons to push me away."

After trying a few times unsuccessfully to respond – and to tell him that I was in love with him, too – I punked out and bolted past him for the door. Part of me expected him to stop me but thankfully (or sadly), he let me go.

By the time I got to my car, the tears were flowing like a waterfall.

CHRISTOPHER WAS STILL out when I got home, and I went straight up to my room, locked the door, and flung myself across the bed. I hadn't felt this ridiculous since the time I put on an uncomfortable outfit and too much makeup for a date with the guy I was into because I thought it would make me more desirable to him. Yet my stubbornly refusing to wear my glasses and stumbling around in tight platform heels didn't make him treat me like any less than the queen he usually did.

And he *still* gave me some prime ding-a-ling that night.

I hated that I couldn't rewind the last hour or so and do things differently. I definitely would have made myself calm down after hearing those women at the gym. And even if I *did* go to Kingston about what I heard, I would have just asked him, not accused him. He deserved better than that, and I knew it.

The shame from my actions wasn't quite as heavy as the revelation that Kingston was in love with me. Even though he'd clearly told me more than once that he was falling for me, it was still a jolt to actually hear it. This beautiful man who had come in and grabbed hold of my attention and heart and refused to give it up without a fight, knocked down every wall I tried to throw up in front of him, was in love with *me*. Regular ol' Adele Mozley.

But with him, I felt anything but regular. He treated me like *I* was the prize of the century. Like *he* was the one who couldn't believe his luck. I knew that any issues I had about Kingston or our relationship were all generated in my own head, because I was scared as hell to give my heart to someone. Especially someone who was younger, hotter, and probably hadn't been disappointed as much as I had when it came to the opposite sex.

With the way I had acted, I would've been surprised if he even wanted to still bother with me. Love or not, maybe he'd decide I just had too many issues. Everybody had a breaking point. And I couldn't expect him to keep putting up with my self-imposed bullshit.

Fresh tears came to my eyes at the thought. I didn't want to lose Kingston. He made me happier than I'd been in years. I hadn't had feelings like this since Nate died. So why couldn't I just tell him that? Or fully accept it?

I heard the front door open and close downstairs, and several moments later, footsteps coming towards my door.

"Ma."

"I'm not trying to be bothered right now, Christopher," I called out wearily, rolling over and placing a hand to my forehead, eyes closed. "You all right?"

"Yes, but-"

"Then *please* just go downstairs or to your room or something and leave me be for a while, okay?"

A few seconds passed before he replied, "All right," and walked off.

I just rolled back over and pulled a pillow over my head.

It didn't take long for me to doze off. When I finally poked my head from underneath my pillows, I squinted at my bedside clock, groping for my glasses. Only about an hour or so had gone by, and when I searched for my phone to check for any messages from Kingston and saw there weren't any, I squeezed my eyes shut. What did I expect? I was the one who had made a fool out of myself; I'd need to be the one to try to fix things, if they could still *be* fixed.

I took my time pushing myself off the bed and trudging to my bathroom to get myself together. After falling asleep in my workout clothes, I didn't exactly smell like a delight. I treated myself to a long, hot shower, then did my usual cocoa butter moisturizing before throwing on some shorts and a tank and heading out of my room, feeling a little better. Christopher was probably hungry, and when my stomach growled, I realized I hadn't eaten anything in hours, myself.

There wasn't any of the usual music coming out of Christopher's room, and when I knocked and poked my head in, it was empty. I could tell the lights were off in the living room when I got to the top of the stairs, and I wondered if he had gone back out. I immediately dismissed that, though, because he had more sense than that. He was probably just knocked out on the couch or something.

But when I got to the bottom of the stairs and heard the moaning and light smooching sounds, I knew that wasn't it. Frowning, I hurried over to turn on the light and immediately heard a voice that certainly didn't belong to my son.

"*Oh my god!*" Zuri screamed, glancing over her shoulder towards me from her position underneath my son on my couch.

"Ma!"

Christopher scrambled to roll off of Zuri, falling to the floor. Zuri, in nothing but her bra and jeans, tried to cover herself. I could see her bra clasp was clumsily halfway undone, and Christopher's pants were unzipped. Before I could even think of stopping myself, I picked up a book from a nearby end table and hurled it at the wall above their heads.

"GET THE HELL OUT OF MY HOUSE!!!" I yelled so hard it made my throat hurt. My hands were shaking as I looked around for something else to throw, and Zuri was screaming and scrambling for her things while Christopher tried to get me to calm down. It was a waste of time. I wanted to rip both their heads off.

"Ma, stop! I'm sorry!" Christopher pleaded with me, standing between me and Zuri while she yanked her shirt over her head and stuffed her feet into her sneakers. "I was trying to ask you if she could come over but you said to leave you alone, and-"

"What, you thought you'd sneak her in here, anyway??"

"Christopher, you told me she said it was okay for me to come over here!" Zuri hissed at him accusingly. "Where are my keys?? Please don't tell my dad about this, Adele! I mean, *Ms.* Adele! I'm sorry!"

I started towards her, but Christopher jumped in front of me. "Ma! I'm sorry; I didn't mean to-"

"*Get that girl out of my house*! And I hope this was worth it 'cause you are gonna be on punishment until the *Lord* comes back!"

"I'm so sorry!" Zuri exclaimed again, scurrying for the door and keeping an eye on me as she did so.

"Ma, can you let me explain, please?"

"Get outta my face, Christopher!" I screamed, losing whatever composure I had left. "There is *nothing* you can say to explain this! You will not be seeing Zuri, Dylan, a basketball, your phone, your computer or anything other than school until I can get past the audacity of you lying and sneaking a girl in here so you could try to *fuck* on my couch! Now *get upstairs!*"

Christopher reared slightly in shock, his skin reddening a little at my anger. The fear in his eyes was evident. I had *never* yelled at him like that.

After he ran upstairs, I just stood there for who knows how long, wishing this stupid day never happened. Everything in me wanted to call Kingston but I couldn't very well go running to him after unfairly giving him the cold shoulder and then accusing him of being unfaithful. I still wasn't ready to talk to Dad. And I knew Rashida was out with Jared.

Just like that, I was crying again.

Chapter 16

"ADELE, HONEY, PLEASE try to calm down."

"Calm down?? My son was probably moments away from having sex on my couch. Don't tell me to calm down."

"It sounded like they were just making out, from what you told me-"

"They had the lights off. His pants were unzipped and her shirt was off. That's not just *making out*."

"Okay, fine; I'm not saying he wasn't wrong. But do you really think catching him fooling around with his girlfriend warranted clearing everything out of his room but the bed and forbidding him from sneezing unless he had your permission?"

"I didn't do all that."

"You did the first part."

"There was no way I wasn't gonna punish him for that, Rashida!"

"I get it," she assured, holding up her hands as she watched me storm back and forth across my bedroom. I had called her and totally interrupted her date with Jared, and when she heard how much I was freaking out, she rushed right over. I'm pretty sure Jared was pissed at me. "He snuck his girl in here, he was probably about to get it in, or at least try to...that's not something I expect you to brush off."

"Good."

"But at least he wasn't doing something worse like drugs or sneaking your wine or watching porn..."

I glared at her. "Is that supposed to make me feel better?"

"Adele, if you can just calm down for a minute and think about all of this." She leaned forward from her seat on my bed, peering at me. "How much of the anger you're feeling right now is really about what's going on with Kingston?"

My hard pacing slowed. I clumsily adjusted my glasses.

"I don't know," I muttered after a few moments.

"Are you sure? If all that drama between you and Kingston hadn't happened mere hours earlier, would you have blown up *this* hard over catching Christopher like that?"

I pushed her question through my head a few times before sighing and dropping my arms. "I guess if I'm honest, probably not."

"So now that you've punished Christopher and I'm sure plan on talking to him once you're thinking rationally again, when are you gonna fix what's going on with you and your man?"

"I...I don't know," I admitted, sulking over to join her on the bed. "I know I messed up and owe him a huge apology. But maybe all of this happened for a reason; maybe Kingston and I are just better off apart."

Rashida looked at me for a few long moments before she hauled off and slapped me.

Actually *slapped* me!

I gaped at her while I held my cheek, not believing she had just done that.

"What the *hell*, Rashida!"

"You're lucky all I *did* was slap you. Maybe somebody knocking some sense into you is what it's going to take for you to quit acting so stupid."

"Excuse me??"

"You're ready to drop this man that you love-"

"I never *said* I loved-"

"Shut up! You know good and well you love that man so don't even waste time acting like you don't."

"Okay, I love him. So??"

"This is the best relationship you've had in years and you're hellbent on throwing it away just because you're scared and hung up on other folks' opinions. Folks that you never call out when they say that bullshit, by the way."

I had no defense to that; I *didn't* usually stand up for myself when people made their comments about me. I just acted like I didn't care then tortured myself about it later. Just like Dad said. How ironic.

"Like I said before, you and I both know that if you ended things with Kingston, you'd be moping around here, miserable and lashing out at everything that moves," Rashida continued. "And you're not gonna keep busting up my dates every time you misplace your anger about it."

"Thanks for being there for me."

"I'm here, aren't I? And you know I'll always have your back but this is something you're doing to *yourself*, girl. You could fix this if you wanted to, because I'm willing to bet Kingston isn't any more ready to end things than you are."

"He hasn't called," I protested with a sniff, wiping the tears that had started streaming from my eyes. "He's probably tired of all my drama by now."

"How do you know? You'd rather sit over here and speculate and jump to conclusions instead of just talking to the man. Doesn't he deserve that? Especially considering that he hasn't actually done anything wrong?"

"Yes." I had to admit that. "Yes, he deserves that."

"So quit this foolishness. Quit torturing yourself. Woman up and call him."

She was right and I knew it. This *was* foolishness. I had messed up and Kingston had been too good to me to not own up to that.

More than anything, I missed Kingston something terrible. I missed how well things were going before that whole mess at my Dad's, which was another person I still hadn't dealt with. But Dad would always be my dad. There was no guarantee that Kingston would remain my man if I kept trying to scrape up reasons to push him away.

AS MUCH AS I WANTED to resolve things with Kingston and I, there was still the matter of Christopher to deal with. I hadn't said anything else to him after banishing him to his room the day before, other than to tell him to move out of the way while I cleared out anything I thought would bring him enjoyment from his room. Now that I had calmed down, I knew I had to talk to him about what happened.

Only problem was, I still didn't know what I was going to say.

Honestly, the image of my son on top of his girlfriend on my couch still lit my torch a little bit. I still couldn't believe their nerve, trying to get their little freak-on in my house with me right upstairs. Ideally, I'd wait until I was *totally* calm. But who knew how long that would take and I couldn't let this fester and drag out.

So after one (or two) fortifying glasses of wine while trying to decide how to approach Christopher, the doorbell rang. Frowning curiously, I quickly rinsed my wineglass and went to the living room. My heart dropped to my knees when I saw Kingston standing there.

"What are you doing here?" I managed to ask, a hand on my pounding chest.

"I'd like for us to talk and finally deal with all this," he stated, eyes on mine. The light breeze outside sent his cologne into the house ahead of him. "May I come in?"

"Of course, yeah," I quickly agreed, stepping aside.

He eyed me as he crossed the threshold, and I quickly noted his brown leather jacket, white tee and dark jeans as I closed the door behind him. Nothing new; he looked as tasty as usual.

Before he could say anything, though, I held up my hands. "Kingston, we absolutely need to talk but first, I have to deal with an issue with Christopher. I was just about to go up and talk to him."

A flash of skepticism narrowed his eyes, but it quickly cleared. "All right, I can respect that. Mind if I ask what's wrong?"

"He..." I shook my head, calming myself. "I caught him and Zuri down here about to have sex last night."

Kingston's eyebrows shot up as his jaw dropped slightly. "What the..."

"Homegirl was shirtless with her bra half off and Christopher's pants were unzipped and ready to be dropped. I admit I totally lost my shit when I saw that; probably scared the girl into never wanting to come back over here. Though I don't totally hate the thought of that."

"Damn. And you haven't talked to Christopher about it at all yet?"

"No. Just took his phone and computer and games and told him to stay in his room. I was way too emotional last night to deal with it, and even now it still kinda sends my blood pressure up, but I can't keep putting it off."

"Understandable. Why don't you let me talk to him?"

I shook my head immediately. "I need to do it; he's *my* child. And even though I'm still a little freaked out, I can't send someone else to do my job just because it's uncomfortable."

Kingston started to say something else, but stopped himself and held up his hands in concession. "All right, then; whatever you say. You already know I'm here to help if you want or need. Go ahead and do your thing; take your time. I'll just hang out down here."

"Thanks," I replied, my nerves returning. I wasn't sure if it was because of the talk I was about to have with Christopher or the talk I was going to have with Kingston after that. This was going to be an emotionally draining evening, I already knew. Glad I didn't drink all the wine.

"Can I give you a piece of advice, though, before you go up there?" Kingston asked, taking my hand.

My face tightened in mild surprise. "Sure, yeah."

"Go in with the intent to listen, and not just accuse. If you go at him guns blazing, he'll be automatically on the defensive and you'll likely get the bare minimum, as far as explanation or response. The conversation won't be anything more than you reprimanding him and the likelihood of him being comfortable coming to you about heavy stuff from here on out will decrease big-time."

"Wow," I mumbled, blinking as I looked at the ground thoughtfully. "I admittedly hadn't thought of it like that..."

"Not trying to tell you what to do," Kingston insisted, kissing my hand before gently releasing it and stepping back. "Just telling you what I know from experience. But you handle it however you think is best."

"Thanks for that," I replied sincerely. "That's probably just what I needed to hear."

"Glad to help."

I watched Kingston remove his jacket and settle in on the couch, then realized I was gazing like some fiend and caught myself. Nervously rubbing my hands over my hips, I made myself go on upstairs.

Christopher's room was quiet when I walked up to his door, and I wondered if he was asleep. Knocking once, I eased the door open. He was curled up on his bed, facing away from me. When he heard me come in, he lifted his head. I noticed his eyes were a little red and it was clear he hadn't brushed his hair.

"We need to talk about what happened, baby," I announced without preamble, closing the door behind me.

Pushing himself into a sitting position, Christopher eyed me warily as I came over to sit at the foot of his bed. "Okay."

Remembering Kingston's advice, I silently counted to five before speaking again. "Can you explain to me why you did what you did?"

"I don't know," he muttered with a hunched shoulder, dropping his eyes to the bed.

"Yes, you do, Christopher."

"I just..." He repeatedly pinched the bedspread with his fingers, not looking at me. "We just kinda got caught up. Like, in the moment or whatever."

"Why was she here?"

"When we got back from the movies, she asked if she could come in and hang out. That's what I had come upstairs to ask you but you said to leave you alone. I guess I should've just told Zuri she had to go, but I lied and said it was okay for her to stay. I didn't even plan to do that; it just came out when I got back downstairs."

I pursed my lips. "And you didn't think I'd find out she was here?"

"We weren't even planning on doing anything; we were just gonna watch TV. But the show we were watching had a couple on there kissing, and Zuri kissed me. And then..." He turned his head, his skin flushing with embarrassment. "Well, you know."

"Right..." I ran a hand through my locs as I processed this information. I admittedly was a little more at ease now than I had been when I'd gone in there. "I'm not gonna lie, I'm pretty disappointed in you, Christopher."

"I know," he grunted, a slight frown puckering his brows. Still wasn't looking at me. "You kinda made that clear with how you screamed at me."

"Well, how would you expect me to react?" I asked, somehow feeling the need to defend myself. "The *last* thing I was expecting was to go downstairs and see that. If I hadn't caught y'all when I did, who knows what you would've done. Of *course* I got angry about that."

"Getting angry is one thing, Ma," he retorted, finally looking up at me with glassy eyes. "But the way you went off, throwing stuff and screaming and cussing, not letting me say anything...you've *never* done that. No matter how bad I messed up. It totally freaked Zuri out. And..." His eyes dropped. "I know I was wrong. But I guess I just never thought you'd come at me like *that*."

I blinked as I took in his words. I'd almost forgotten about the book I threw at them. It had just been a gut reaction; I didn't even think about it. But that didn't make it right, and I knew it. If I had messed around and hit Zuri, there would have been no justification. Regardless, neither of them deserved that.

"I'll admit that I crossed a line with the throwing," I finally admitted. "That was...that was wrong of me. And I shouldn't have screamed the way I did, especially at Zuri. I could've handled things better but I won't apologize for getting angry or punishing you."

"I get that I deserve to be punished. But that still hurt. Then you ignored me for a whole day after taking all my stuff. It's just..." He sighed, his shoulders slumping before he leaned back against the headboard, looking at the ceiling. "This is one of those times I wish Dad was still here. *He* would understand."

Hearing that made tears sting my eyes. "Baby, I know you miss your dad. But you can still talk to me about stuff. Nothing has to change about that."

"It's not the same, Ma. That's why I like Kingston so much; he's cool and easy to talk to but still tells me the real deal. But not like he's lecturing or talking down to me. I like that."

"I see." That kinda stung a little bit. I thought Christopher and I were close enough that we could talk about anything. But apparently not.

A few awkward moments passed before I ventured, "So if I asked if you and Zuri have had sex..."

"Ma!" he whined.

"It's a perfectly logical question, Christopher, considering what I caught y'all doing. You remember what I said about condoms and-"

"Oh my *gosh*..."

"What's the problem? It's not like we've never talked about sex before."

"Ma, can we not? I just...I really can't talk about this with you."

Well, damn. Christopher and I had had the sex talk a few times over the years, and while he was never gung-ho about it, he never shut it down like he was doing now. I didn't know what the difference was, but then again, I had never been a teenage boy.

Fortunately, there was someone downstairs who had been.

With a sigh of defeat, I looked over at him. "So I guess I don't have to ask if you'd be more comfortable talking to Kingston about all this."

Christopher's eyes lit up. "Can I? You're giving me my phone back?"

"*Hell* no. But he's downstairs. I can ask him to come up, if you want."

"That'd be cool." He paused and shot me a wary glance. "Are...you gonna stay while he's in here?"

Another kick to the chest. "No, Christopher. If it'll make you that uncomfortable, I leave you two alone."

His relief was obvious. "Good."

Figuring I'd gotten all the information out of Christopher that I was gonna get, I stood and headed for the door. At least he had acknowledged that he was wrong.

I didn't bother trying to think of anything else to say; I just walked out. Part of me hoped that Christopher would stop me and give me another nugget of information, even if it was a small one. Or tell me he loved me to my back. But he said nothing. I guess things really had changed.

Sulking down the stairs, I found Kingston kicked back on the couch, scrolling through his phone. When he saw me, he sat up.

"How'd it go?"

I shrugged, plopping into the armchair. "Could've been worse, I guess."

"Did he explain himself?"

"Yeah, he did that much. But that was about it."

"What do you mean?"

"Other than letting me know why he had Zuri in here and acknowledging that he was wrong for it – oh, and letting me know that my reaction to finding them like I did freaked them out – he was pretty tight-lipped."

"What else did you want him to say, babe?"

Him calling me that only reminded me that we still had our own issues to talk about. "I don't know. I was trying to dig a little deeper but he got super uncomfortable. That's when he mentioned how much he likes talking to you."

A smile twitched the corner of his lips. "Yeah?"

"Mmm-hmm. And when I let him know you were here and offered to send you up there, he got all happy and agreed, of course making sure I'd leave you two alone since apparently he can only talk to me about certain stuff now."

I might've been making it sound worse than it was. But I was hurt, damn it.

"I already know you're taking that some kinda way but I really wish you wouldn't," Kingston surmised. "I got to a point where there were certain things I couldn't talk to my mother about, too, and we were as thick as thieves. Doesn't mean I didn't love her or value our relationship. There's just certain stuff a woman can't relate to, that's all, no matter how much she wants to."

"Yeah," I grudgingly acknowledged, wringing the hem of my shirt. "I can understand that, I guess."

"You're really good with me going up there?"

"Yeah. If you don't mind, that is."

"Of course not."

He placed a warm hand on my shoulder as he passed, heading for the stairs. I knew I should've been grateful for Kingston being there for Christopher, especially since Nate was no longer here. And grateful that Kingston was so willing to be there for my son, as well.

I turned on the television to try to distract myself from wondering what was going on upstairs. My imagination was all over the place, wondering if Christopher was telling Kingston about sneaking off with Zuri when he told me he was going to his friend Dylan's, or that he and Zuri had been getting it in for months. Hell, maybe he was telling Kingston that he had accidentally knocked Zuri up and was too scared to tell me. Oh my gosh, I wasn't ready to be a grandmother!

As I was imagining screaming triplets and where I could find the best deals on diapers, Kingston and Christopher came back downstairs. I turned towards them in surprise; they hadn't been up there as long as I expected them to be.

"Y'all done already?" I marveled, eying them as they filed to the couch.

"Not quite," Kingston replied, glancing at Christopher. "We talked about some things, but I also let him know that it would be good for the three of us to talk together, too."

"Really?"

"Kingston said that I can always come to him, but that I can't shut you out," Christopher piped up, somewhat grudgingly. "That there's some stuff you deserve to know about as my mother, even if it's kinda weird to talk about."

Smiling gratefully at Kingston, I felt my heart swell for this man. He always considered me. Why in the world had I ever allowed the thought of letting him go enter my mind??

Just like that, I was anxious to get Christopher out of the room so Kingston and I could hash things out. It hit me just how much I'd missed him while I'd been acting stubborn and stupid.

But first, the three of us had a lengthy talk about some things. Kingston told us about how his high school girlfriend had snuck him into her room when he was around Christopher's age, and he had to hide in the closet when her father came home early. By the time the girl's father went to the bathroom and Kingston had the chance to make a break for it, he was so scared that he never tried anything like that again.

"And I *still* haven't told my mama about that," Kingston admitted. "It was pretty embarrassing. My favorite uncle knew about it, though, since he lived nearby and it was his house I ran to. He got on my ass good enough, and made me come over every Saturday morning for the next two months to cut his grass and help him around the house. After that, I was good on the sneaking around."

"Why can't you tell your mama about it now, though?" I asked him, amused. "You're in your thirties..."

"Yeah, I'm in my thirties but she'd probably still try to punish me some kind of way just for keeping it from her all these years. Especially since I was supposed to be on punishment at the time and had lied to her, saying I was staying after school to work on a project. I had to beg my uncle – her brother – not to tell her, either."

"Wow," Christopher chuckled behind his fist. "That's wild, Kingston."

"Oh, that's not even *half* of the stupid stuff I did back in the day. And most of it was me trying to do grown stuff before I was ready." His eyes turned serious as he looked at Christopher. "Stay in your lane, homie. It's natural to be curious and have urges about some things. But remember that there are some things you can't undo once they're done."

Christopher looked down at his knees and nodded.

"I know at least three students at my school who are getting ready to become parents before they're even done being kids, and they all wish they could go back and make different choices. You want that to be you?"

"No sir," Christopher quickly responded, shaking his head aggressively. "Not at all. I don't want any babies any time soon."

"Don't do anything to make any, then," Kingston ordered. "'Cause even when you think you're being careful, things can still happen. And not even just pregnancy; there are all kinds of sexually transmitted diseases, some of which can't be cured."

"True..."

"You're young, dude. Just enjoy it. Being an adult will come soon enough. And trust, you'll miss this young and carefree time when it's gone."

I eyed Christopher as he took in Kingston's words. Kingston's advice was similar to things I had told Christopher myself at times, but I guess it was different coming from someone else.

We all talked for a while longer, culminating in Christopher apologizing to me for what he did and promising to do better. I appreciated that, and let him know I was sorry for flying off the handle the way I had, and for not listening to him.

"You're still punished, though," I made sure to emphasize, smirking at him.

"I know," Christopher replied with a smile. He stood. "I'll go back to my room now, if that's all right."

"Yeah, it's fine."

"Thanks for the help, Kingston," he said, giving him some pound. "I appreciate it. Hope you stick around for a while. A long while."

"I certainly plan to," Kingston replied, looking right at me. I felt my whole body tighten.

Go upstairs, Christopher.

As soon as Christopher was out of the room, I dove on Kingston, kissing him like a madwoman. He responded immediately, wrapping his arms around me and returning the kiss with equal urgency and intensity. He had missed me as much as I missed him. But this wasn't enough. I needed the whole shebang.

"Let's go upstairs," I whispered against his lips as I rubbed my body against his.

"I thought we were supposed to be talking about us," he reminded me as his hands slid all around my ass.

"We are." I sucked on his neck, making him moan. I loved doing that. "And we will. But I need you to scratch this itch first."

"Adele..."

"I know we have stuff to work out," I acknowledged, sitting up slightly. "And I'm not trying to avoid that. But one thing I'm absolutely sure of is that I don't want to lose you. I'm sorry for acting like I did; you didn't deserve any of that."

He looked up at me, his fingertips grazing up and down my back.

"I-I love you, Kingston," I made myself tell him. My hand caressed his beautiful face. "More than I thought I could or would, and I admit that scares me. But I don't wanna run from it anymore."

"You don't have anything to be afraid of, babe," he assured, catching my hand and kissing it. "This is where I wanna be. *With you* is where I wanna be. And I'm glad you love me 'cause I damn sure love you."

He pulled my face to his and we tongued each other down, going at it like a couple of horndogs. It was several minutes later when I finally composed myself enough to pull him upstairs to my room so we could *really* go at it. I needed some of that prime ding-a-ling.

Chapter 17

KINGSTON STRODE INTO his bedroom in nothing but his briefs, carrying a tray of waffles, fruit, and bacon. I grinned as I sat up in bed, putting on my glasses.

"Nothing hotter than a fine-ass man bringing me food," I stated, eying him lustfully. "Thank you, Hot Cakes."

He chuckled, laying the tray on the bed. I still didn't know if he liked my new pet name for him or not but he never tripped about it, if he didn't. "My fine-ass woman deserves it. What do you want to drink?"

"Milk."

"Nice try."

"Oh come on..."

"I'm not giving you anything that's going to keep you in the bathroom for hours. Forget it."

"It won't be that bad. And look, you have butter, here."

"It's vegan and I don't even expect you to eat any. And you hate almond milk, you hate soy milk, you said you didn't like the lactose-free stuff I got you that time, so..."

"Do you have any of that now?"

"Yeah. Why, you want some?"

"Please. Maybe I can try to choke it down. You know how I am about fake dairy."

"I do," he chuckled, shaking his head. "I'll be right back."

I snuck a piece of bacon while he went to get our drinks, sighing as I leaned on the pillows against the headboard. I couldn't remember the last time I'd been so happy.

It had been about a month since our reconciliation, and things were awesome. We were all over each other, and I never got tired of him using that L-word. There had only been one or two times when that familiar doubt about us started to creep in, but thankfully I managed to stomp it out before it could catch fire. I had a good man who was with me because he wanted to be, and who I wanted to be with just as much, and I was done trying to sabotage or question it.

Once he returned with my perpetrating milk and juice for himself, he climbed into bed with me and we proceeded to grub on the breakfast he made.

"Christopher still at your dad's?" Kingston asked, spreading the fake butter on his waffles.

"Yeah. He'll be over there another week. Part bonding, part punishment. Christopher said Dad is working him like a Hebrew slave."

Kingston laughed. "Well, hopefully all of this will make him pause the next time he's tempted to go out of pocket."

"Hopefully. I don't expect him to be perfect; just have to be ready to deal with it whenever he does slip up."

"He will. It's just part of life. We'll be there for him regardless. Messing up doesn't stop at any certain age, anyway."

"I've certainly proven that recently."

"All in the past, babe," he reminded me, rubbing my thigh through the sheet. "We're good now."

I smiled, briefly placing my head on his shoulder. "And I'm going to make sure it stays that way."

"Music to my ears." He kissed my forehead. "And I meant to tell you, I'm proud of you for finally talking to your dad."

I shrugged, biting off another piece of bacon. Oh how I *loved* bacon. "It needed to be done, even though I didn't expect it to really change anything. I let him know what I heard him say about me back in the day, and how certain comments he makes now makes me feel, and he didn't really have a lot to say; he certainly didn't apologize or give me any kind of reassurance. Just gave me this long look before grunting and going back to his puzzle."

"Well, at least he knows. Maybe he's the kind of person who can't admit when he's wrong."

"There's no 'maybe' about it. That's exactly how he is."

"Regardless, you got it off your chest, and that's the important thing. And I can tell you feel a lot better since that conversation; you haven't been as tense."

"You're right. I needed to unburden myself of that, but more importantly, I had to stop worrying about what he thinks, anyway. Him or anybody else. I sincerely love myself as is so, respectfully, fuck them."

He smiled, then bit his lip as he eyed me up and down. "*Shit*, you're turning me on right now."

My grin was automatic. He was already easing down the sheet that was covering my breasts. "Yeah? Let's move this tray out of the way, then, and do something about that."

LATER ON THAT EVENING, we took a shower together then hurried to get dressed.

"You know we're gonna be late," I muttered, trying to put on my heels and fasten my bracelet at the same time.

"Don't blame me, Ms let's-go-one-more-round."

"I wouldn't be so greedy with the ding-a-ling if it wasn't so good. So it *is* kinda your fault."

"Uh-huh." He was smiling, though, tying his tie.

"And need I remind you that you hoisted me onto the bathroom counter and kept your face between my legs after we got out of the shower. We wouldn't be rushing if it wasn't for that."

"You complaining?" He smirked at me, his brow cocked.

"Hell no. Rashida will be all right."

"Hopefully she won't cuss me out too bad for us getting to her engagement party a few minutes late."

"Please, she's had a first class seat on cloud nine ever since Jared proposed a couple of weeks ago. She probably won't even notice we're not there yet."

Chuckling, Kingston quickly removed his wave cap and inspected his black shiny waves in the mirror. "Wonder why they're getting married so quick. She's not pregnant, is she?"

"If she is, she hasn't told me. They just don't want a long engagement; they want to be man and wife more than they want to spend months and months wedding planning."

"I can understand that." He glanced at me in the mirror and opened his mouth to say something else, but stopped himself and put on his watch.

A few minutes later, we rushed out the door and headed across town to the restaurant where Rashida and Jared were holding their engagement party. Kingston and I entered the already-full banquet room hand-in-hand, and Rashida immediately rushed over to us.

"Girl, you're not supposed to come up in here looking hotter than me! I swear I need some of those boobs!"

"Stop," I laughed.

"Need I bother asking why y'all are late?" she asked with a teasing glint in her eye and a hand on her hip.

Kingston chuckled while I winked at her. "No. You needn't."

"Horny asses. But I'll let it go because I love seeing my girl so happy. But you better not do anything to hurt her, Kingston, I ain't playing. I'll kick your ass. Don't think I can't do it."

"Hey, I got you," Kingston assured, holding up his free hand. "You don't have to worry about that. Adele is the most important person in my life; there's no way I'd willingly do anything to hurt her."

Rashida grinned, looking back and forth between us. "I love it. Maybe we'll be having an event like this for the two of *you* one day."

Before I could even gauge Kingston's reaction to that, Jared came up and wrapped his arms around Rashida from behind.

"Hey, glad y'all could make it," he said to me and Kingston, beaming. Both he and Rashida had been like walking glow sticks ever since he put that ring on her finger.

"No problem; thanks for having us," Kingston replied as they bumped fists.

"Before I forget, Jared, I need to give you the you-hurt-my-friend-and-I'll-kill-you speech," I reminded him.

Rashida's smile widened as she craned her neck to look up at Jared, who only nodded knowingly. "I figured that was coming. Do we need to step out on the patio or something real quick?"

"No, that was it."

They all laughed at me as if I was kidding.

"Bro, I just got the same from your fiancée," Kingston told Jared, his arm sliding around my waist and pulling me closer. I loved when he did that. Rashida took note of my automatic swoon and grinned, winking at me. I winked back.

The four of us stood there talking for another couple of minutes before the betrothed couple went off to greet more guests. Kingston and I wandered around the room as I introduced him to my and Rashida's mutual friends and her parents. He was so smooth, falling into a natural rapport with everybody he met. I was the proudest thing walking, having him on my arm.

Of course, he drew plenty of attention from the single ladies in the room. Hell, even the not-single ladies. Kingston was hot, and got looks just about every time we went anywhere together. He didn't ever seem to notice, though (and believe me, I paid attention to that) and always had eyes only for me. Thankfully I was past the point of worrying about him seeing someone he'd think was more aesthetically suited for him than I was. He liked my forty-five year old, near-sighted, plush-bodied self just as it was and I was finally confident in that.

One guest that I didn't expect to see was Bradley. I noticed him when we were all sitting down to eat, but had no plans of speaking. I wasn't tripping over what happened between us anymore, but we had nothing to talk about. He was there with a deep brown-skinned beauty who seemed intent on making it clear to everyone that the two of them were there together, the way she never seemed to want to let go of his arm. Bradley caught my eye at the table and gave me a smile and a nod, which I politely returned before turning my attention elsewhere.

All through dinner, dessert, drinks and Rashida and Jared's speeches and toasts, I could feel Bradley's eyes on me. I don't know what the fascination was; we hadn't spoken in months. I couldn't imagine he was salty about my blocking him; it's not like we had been in a relationship. And he had clearly moved on, so I wished he'd keep his eyes on his own date instead of worrying about me.

"Why is your boy eyeing me so much?" I asked Rashida in a low voice when we had a brief moment alone. We both held glasses of champagne.

Rashida glanced around the room before turning her light brown eyes back to me. "Who?"

"Bradley."

"Oh. Yeah, I forgot to tell you he was gonna be here. My bad."

"I don't care about him being here; I just wish he'd quit staring. If I didn't know better, I'd think he wants to talk to me or something."

"He probably does. I know he's asked me about you a couple of times after you blocked him."

My brow arched curiously, mildly surprised by that. "And you said?"

"I said if you wanted to talk to him, you would. And that I wasn't getting in the middle of it."

"Hmph. Well, whatever."

Rashida looked at me and squeezed my arm. "I'm so proud of you, girl."

"Proud of me? For what?"

"All these women in here with googly eyes for your man and you're not freaking out. If this was a few months ago, you'd be super paranoid about one of them catching Kingston's eye."

"True."

"But now, you're not even bothered. All secure and shit. I love it."

"Kingston has done a good job proving to me who it is he wants. I know my Hot Cakes isn't going anywhere."

"Did you just say Hot Cakes?"

"Shut up." I looked across the room at Kingston talking to Jared. He apparently sensed I was looking at him and turned his eyes to me, giving me a sexy wink. I grinned, feeling warm with both the love and the lust I had for him. "What do you call Jared?"

"In public, I keep it simple with sweetie, bae, honey butt; stuff like that. Now if you wanna know what I call him in *private-*"

"Never mind; *honey butt* will suffice. Anyway, if Kingston *did* choose to leave and be with somebody else, then to hell with him. I won't act like it won't hurt, but I can't make myself and him crazy constantly worrying about stuff I have no control over."

"Hell, you were making *me* crazy, too."

"Hush."

"But for real, I'm so happy for the two of you. You deserve a man like Kingston, who adores you like he does. And he better know how lucky he is to have *you*."

I blinked back emotion as I leaned in and hugged her. "Thanks for that, sis."

Rashida was summoned by her parents, so I looked back over to Kingston. He was still talking to Jared and a few other guys, so I decided to step out to the patio for some air. Grabbing a fresh glass of bubbly, I slipped outside, immediately loving how the cool night air felt.

After just a couple of minutes, I heard the patio doors open behind me.

"I finally get a minute with you."

Closing my eyes for a moment and sighing, I took my time turning around. "What's up, Bradley?"

He looked the same. Still admittedly cute. Smelled good, as always. But I felt nothing.

Sliding a hand in his pocket, he eyed me as he approached. I crossed one arm over my chest and sipped champagne with my other hand, resisting the urge to step back.

"If I didn't know better, I'd think you were avoiding me."

"No need for that."

"You're looking good. Looking *great*, really." His eyes roamed my body in my red strapless tube dress, something that I never would have had the nerve to wear a few months earlier. But it accentuated all my good parts, and I felt damn sexy in it. And Kingston couldn't keep his hands off my ass when I wore this thing.

"Thank you."

"I was hoping you'd be here tonight," Bradley stated, resting a hand on one of the nearby wrought iron chairs. "I've been wanting to ask why you ghosted me the way you did."

I threw up a dismissive hand. "Water under the bridge by now, right?"

"Not to me. I thought we were better than that."

"Hmph."

"I mean, you said we were cool after what happened on our date-"

"Bradley," I interjected, shaking my head. "What does it matter now? That was months ago. I've moved on, you've moved on. No need in dredging up old stuff."

"What if I said I've been missing you, though?"

Before I could respond to that nonsense, Bradley's date joined us on the patio, shooting daggers at me.

"There you are," she crooned to Bradley while throwing me an accusing glare. She took hold of his arm with both hands. "I was looking for you."

"Just catching up with a friend. Adele, this is my date, Lydia Montello. Lydia, Adele Mozley."

"Montello as in Montello Mustard," Lydia was quick to emphasize. "We're in stores all across the country. I'm sure you've heard of it. My father's picture is on the bottle. People say he's the spitting image of Denzel."

My eyebrows shot up in feigned fascination. "Wow, he's got it like that and chose to go into the *mustard* business?"

Bradley coughed back a laugh, and Lydia glared at him.

"But no, can't say I've heard of you all," I continued, taking a sip from my glass. "But I'll try to keep that in mind the next time I'm in the mood for a hot dog."

"Shouldn't be too long then, I bet," she retorted, sweeping her eyes over me. "I imagine you eat your share of them."

"Lydia..." Bradley warned.

"I'm actually more into burgers," I replied, unfazed. "And to keep it real with you, girl, I was just trying to be polite; I don't even *like* mustard. But good for y'all on the success and everything. Black-owned business for the win."

"And what is it *you* do?" Lydia quizzed. Bradley's lips were quivering, trying to control his laughter.

"Activities Director at a senior facility."

"Ugh, working around old people all day?" She actually shuddered. "I couldn't even do that."

"Well you don't *need* to do that, with your family rolling in mustard and everything, right?"

Her eyes tightened as the doors opened behind them. Bradley and Lydia turned to see Kingston standing there.

"Excuse me," he said politely before stepping around them and coming over to me. He placed his hands on my waist. "You good, babe? I didn't know where you went."

"Yeah, I'm great; just came out to get some air." I smiled up at him as I placed a hand on his chest. Nodding towards the couple staring at us curiously, I gently turned Kingston to face them. "Sweetie, this is Bradley and Lydia."

"Bradley and Lydia, nice to meet y'all," Kingston stated, stepping over to shake each of their hands. "I'm Kingston, Adele's man."

"Kingston," Lydia purred, not even trying to hide her appreciation as she eyed him up and down.

Bradley's amusement from moments before was now out the window as he semi-glared at Kingston. When Kingston eased behind me and started casually sliding his hands around my hips, Bradley took notice, his eyes tightening.

"How long have you two been...together?" he asked us, his voice suddenly gruff.

"A while," I replied, my free hand reaching back to grab Kingston's thigh. Bradley's skin actually looked like it was turning red.

"But not long enough," Kingston added, making me grin like a schoolgirl. "What about you two?"

"We've just gone out a few times," Bradley answered before Lydia could. "Still getting to know each other."

"Lock that down, man, if she's who you want," Kingston advised, his arms encircling my waist and squeezing. "Don't drag your feet. You know what they say about another man's trash being another man's treasure. It's a bitch living with regrets."

Lydia looked up at Bradley expectantly as Bradley gazed at me. He looked like he wanted to say something but before he could, Kingston turned my face to his and gave me a lingering kiss, no doubt sending Bradley's blood pressure into the clouds. I was actually kinda giddy at the thought.

"Babe, I'm about ready to head out, if you are," Kingston told me, brushing some locs from my eyes. "And Rashida wants to see you before we leave."

"Okay. I'm about partied out, anyway. Plus I'm about ready to get out of these shoes."

"And I'm about ready to get you out of that dress," Kingston whispered, his lips grazing my ear. I squealed and playfully swatted him on the shoulder before taking his hand.

"You two enjoy the rest of your night," I said to Bradley and Lydia as I led Kingston past them off the patio.

"Nice meeting you, *Kingston*," Lydia stated pointedly, ignoring me.

I stopped and turned to her, giving her a look that showed I wasn't playing. "Don't keep trying it, girl. I'd hate to have to show my ass in here 'cause you wanna keep flirting with my man. You don't want these problems."

Lydia reared back in shock and Kingston and I walked back into the banquet room.

"You know I love it when you make it known who I belong to like that," Kingston informed, gently tugging on my hand to get me to stop walking. He lustfully eyed me up and down as he bit his lip. "That's fucking *sexy*."

"I'm not trying to share you with anybody," I insisted, grabbing the sides of his suit jacket and stealing a kiss.

"Oh, babe, you don't even have to worry about that. All this is for you." He pulled me close and slid his hands around to my ass. "Is all this for me?"

"Kingston!" I hissed with a smile, pushing his hands away. "At least wait until we get outside!"

"Answer the question, woman."

"It absolutely is all for you."

"That's what I wanna hear. Now let's hurry up and get home so I can get at you 'cause that dress is *killing* me right now."

"As soon as we say good-bye to Rashida and Jared, I'm all yours."

About twenty minutes later, we were barely to the car before Kingston yanked me to him and laid a deep, hard kiss on me. His hands roamed all over my body as he backed me against the passenger door.

"Kingston..." I gasped as his hand squeezed my breast.

"You said I only had to wait until we got outside, right?" he breathlessly reminded me, his other hand grabbing the side of my face as he ran a tongue around my ear and down my neck, causing me to shudder violently.

"I did..." I pulled his hard groin closer and enjoyed the feeling of him gently grinding against me while I held handfuls of his ass. "But we should probably at least get in the car before we put on a show out here."

"Let 'em watch."

His thumb grazed my nipple through my dress and I almost lost it. And when he slid one of my breasts out and began running his tongue around it, I legit forgot we were outside for a moment; I just held his head in both hands, groaning and writhing like a madwoman as he sucked one nipple and played with the other right out there in the open.

"Shit, I'm about to cum..." I whispered, my head falling back. My fingers tensed on the back of his neck.

"Come on," he urged, rolling that magic tongue of his. I heard people somewhere in the distance but neither of us cared. I was too close to stop.

"Yes, Kingston, yes..." My face pinched in pleasure, the experience heightened by the awareness that people could probably see us. I didn't have time to be self-conscious about it, though, because when that orgasm it, it hit hard, and it was all I could do to not let out the scream I wanted to.

"Aaaugh!" I gasped, my mouth falling open as pleasure shock waves zapped throughout my body. I held Kingston's head in a vise grip to my chest, unable to move or speak for several moments. He just gripped my waist, letting me ride it out before he stood and kissed my lips, moaning and whispering how sexy that was.

"That's my girl," he grunted against my lips.

My hands gripped his shirt as our tongues started to play together. I usually needed some recovery time after an orgasm but I felt myself wanting more already. Maybe it was the exhibitionism of fooling around and having my whole titties out on display outside. Whatever it was, I wasn't fighting it.

Before I had him hike my dress up and bend me over the hood, I gently pushed him back, pulling the top of my dress back up. Chest heaving, I ordered, "Take me home and step on it."

My eyes clearly relaying what I wanted, Kingston quickly unlocked the door and let me in before practically running around to his side. We screeched out of the parking lot, passing Bradley and Lydia, who were gaping at us with their jaws on the pavement. I just grinned and waved. Guess they saw us.

We got back to Kingston's house in record time and were barely through the door before clothes started coming off. First thing being my dress.

"*Damn*, Adele," Kingston moaned, gripping my ass as I rode him on the couch. He lifted his hips to meet mine, matching my rhythm. His eyes closed as his head fell against the back of the couch, pulling his bottom lip between his teeth. "Ride that shit, baby. I swear I can't get enough of you..."

I have to admit, I felt like some kind of superwoman right then, making this hunk of a man writhe and shudder like he was. I braced my hands against his hard chest as I worked my hips over him, switching up my bouncing and rotating and grinding so much that it made him want to explode. When he finally hollered my name at the top of his lungs, squeezing me around my waist with both arms and burying his face in my breasts, I rested my cheek on top of his head and sighed in tired contentment.

"You're gonna wear me out," I informed him, running my hands along his sweaty back.

"You can handle it." He planted wet tongue kisses on my breasts, sending a shiver through me. He gave me that half-mast post-sex look that always shot a lightning bolt right to my lady parts. "Your sex drive is damn near higher than mine."

"Vitamins work."

"Remind me to get you a lifetime supply. Tomorrow."

A phone started ringing from across the room, and we both glanced in the general direction.

"That yours or mine?" he muttered, still nibbling on my slick skin.

"Mine, I think," I replied, reluctantly untangling myself from Kingston's embrace and going over to get my phone from my purse. "Oh crap..."

"What's wrong?" he asked, watching as I hastily yanked on his dress shirt.

"It's Christopher."

"Is it a video call?"

"No, but I don't want to talk to my son while I'm naked." I tossed his underwear to him. "Put these back on."

He shook his head but did as I asked. Once we were both covered, I answered the phone, putting it on speakerphone.

"Hey, baby."

"Hey, Ma," Christopher's voice filled the living room. It seemed a little deeper than the last time we talked. "You with Kingston?"

"Yep. We just got back from Auntie Rashida's engagement party. He can hear you; I've got you on speaker."

"Oh. Hey, Kingston."

"What's up, man?" Kingston greeted him. "You good? How's it going over there with your granddad?"

"It's okay but I'm ready to come home. He keeps finding more and more stuff for me to do."

I chuckled. "What was the task today?"

"Writing 'I will not disobey my mama' a thousand times. A *thousand*! It took me forever. My hand feels like it's gonna fall off."

Kingston and I laughed. Dad used to make me do that back in the day when I messed up, too.

"Sounds about right," I agreed.

"Believe me, I've learned my lesson. And anyway, part of the reason I'm over here isn't even an issue anymore."

Kingston and I glanced at each other in confusion. "What do you mean?" Kingston asked.

"I broke up with Zuri," Christopher announced.

I actually started to applaud but Kingston nudged me. "Really? Did something happen?"

"She thinks she knows everything just 'cause she's older than me. I got tired of her always trying to tell me what to do; she actually argued with me about what I wanna do for my birthday next month. And I don't want a girlfriend I'm always fussing with."

It was a good thing we were on the phone so I didn't have to hide my grin. Zuri seemed like a nice enough girl but I didn't like her for my son. I was thrilled that he finally realized that she wasn't right for him for himself.

"Are you okay?" I still had to ask.

"I'm fine. I think I'm gonna lay off girls for a while. They're too much trouble."

Kingston and I snickered. I figured I'd wait a while before trying to dispute that.

We all talked for a few more minutes before Christopher said he had to go to bed. I ended the call and looked over at Kingston with a sigh. He chuckled again.

"You know you haven't stopped grinning since he said he broke up with his girl, right?"

"You smile about stuff you're happy about."

He shook his head. "Well, he'll be all right. There'll probably be plenty more girls in his future before it's all said and done."

"Ugh."

"Hey, I have a question," he hedged, lifting my legs onto his lap.

"Okay..."

"Who is Bradley to you? Is he your ex or something?"

I sucked my teeth. "No. I liked him but he promptly friend-zoned me."

"Well he seems to regret that, the way he was looking at you tonight."

"Not my problem."

"Hell, I should thank him. If he was smart enough to realize what he had, you wouldn't be with me."

"Everything happens for a reason," I grinned at him, leaning in for a kiss that he quickly obliged me.

The kiss lingered for a few moments, then Kingston leaned his head against the back of the couch, his eyes roaming my face. I could see the adoration in them and it made me feel warm and tingly all over. I couldn't see myself ever getting tired of that look from him.

"Babe," he finally said, clearing his throat. His hands nervously slid up and down my legs. "Let me ask you something else..."

I sat up a little, looking at him curiously.

"Do you...can you see yourself with me a year from now? Five years from now? Beyond that?"

My smile faded a tiny bit, only because the question caught me off guard. "Oh..."

"I'm not trying to freak you out, babe, but...I want to be your husband one day. I want to be a father to Christopher. I want it to be you and me until there's nothing else. That's how much I love you, Adele; I swear I've never felt this for anyone else."

The weight of his words hit me, sending tears to my eyes. "Kingston..."

He reached over and lovingly swiped my tears with his thumbs. "I understand if you're not there yet. But I had to let you know where I was and what my intentions are. If I have my way, you're *going* to be my wife."

"Wow," I breathed, my hands covering my mouth. All kinds of emotions were slamming into each other at once in my head and heart. The tears started coming faster as Kingston's words began rolling like ticker tape through my mind.

"Did I overstep with that?" he asked, gently grabbing my wrist. "I'm sorry if I-"

"No, no," I stopped him, shaking my head vigorously and sending my locs across my face. The hand of the wrist he was holding caressed his face, gazing at him in adoration. I couldn't believe I was blessed enough to have a man like him. And not just because he was younger and hotter; it was because he truly cherished and valued me. That kind of thing was priceless, and so much more important than anything physical.

"You didn't overstep at all," I assured him, sniffling and smiling. "I'm just floored right now, but in...the best way. Kingston, baby, I love you *so* much, and there have been plenty of times where I laid in bed and fantasized about us in the future, but I never thought..."

"You never thought what?" he urged gently.

"I never thought you'd want the same thing. At least, not indefinitely. I was just going to be happy with how we are for however long it lasted."

"Babe..." He grabbed the front of my shirt and pulled me closer. When we were nose-to-nose, he lifted my chin and kissed me, moving my locs from my face. "I'm not going anywhere. I can't predict the future but I know what I want. You have all of my heart. And I can't imagine going forward without you next to me. I want you, Adele. All of you. Indefinitely."

"I want that, too."

He smiled, looking so ridiculously sexy and adorable and everything else that it was unfair.

"You sure?"

"Am I sure that I want to be Mrs. Adele Farrell one day? No doubt in my mind."

"Babe," he breathed, practically tackling me. He grabbed both sides of my face as we kissed deeply and intently, forgetting about everything else. My legs encircled his waist as I tried to hold him as close to me as possible, because I knew I never wanted to let this man go.

"You're exquisite," he whispered against my lips, a thumb stroking my chin while his other hand lifted my leg higher around him. "Please know that. I thank God for you. You're priceless to me, Adele. And I'm never gonna let you forget it."

Thanks so much for reading! I hope you enjoyed reading about Adele and Kingston's story as much as I enjoyed writing it. I actually turned down social activities to stay in and work on this. Maybe I'm a nerd. *shrug*

And did you notice the brief cameo from a *Split By the Bell* and *The Karma Call* character and location in there? No?? Then maybe you should go back and read those, too. *wink wink nudge nudge*

If you liked this story, please consider leaving a review. And if you want to show *extra* love, share that you read it on social media. I love to see it! ☺

You can find me on Instagram and TikTok at @authorjessicaterry and on Twitter at @itsJessicaTerry. And don't forget to go to jessicaterry.com and get your free novel.

Also by Jessica Terry

Some Like 'em Thick
It's All Right...Now
Not By a Long Shot
Get Right
Decisions and Consequences
Take One For the Team
When You Share Too Much
Backtalk
Emasculated
Restless
The Beginning of Again
Always and Nevers
She is Me
Split By the Bell
The Karma Call
Forehead Kiss
All Because of Ava
<u>The Introvert Series</u>
An Introvert's Christmas
Wooing the Introvert
The Introvert Roast
I, Take Thee Introvert
The Introvert Series Compilation (paperback only)

Discussion Questions

1. Adele was used to getting friend-zoned by men. Do you think she used humor as a defense mechanism, to mask her embarrassment and hurt? Or did you think she was just being herself?

2. After her humiliating experience with Bradley, do you think Adele overreacted in how she handled it?

3. What do you think of how Kingston approached Adele in the restaurant?

4. Do you feel Adele was leaning on Christopher too much for company?

5. Speaking of Christopher, do you think Adele was unreasonable or unfair with the girls he brought home?

6. Did you get the feeling that Adele was jealous of Rashida?

7. What did you think of Stuart, Adele's dad? Was he wrong in saying the things he said about Adele?

8. Do you think Kingston was out of line, giving Christopher his number without running it by Adele? What about with the advice he gave Adele on how to deal with him?

9. Kingston showed Adele a pretty humbling flaw of his. Do you think this was a turning point for her?

10. Adele kept harping on Kingston's age and said his looks were "almost intimidating." Yet she constantly insisted she didn't have self-esteem issues. Do you

agree with her or do you think she was fooling herself?

11. Do you think Adele's pet name for Kingston was insensitive, given his deformity?

Did you love *Love Intolerant*? Then you should read *All Because of Ava*[1] by Jessica Terry!

[2]

Ava and Harper's honeymoon phase came to a screeching halt as soon as she met Mario.

Ava battled with the guilt of fantasizing about one man while being married to another...even if the one she was married to increasingly felt like a stranger the more she learned about him.

Mario knew Ava was taken, but that didn't stop him from wanting her. And when he and Ava keep getting thrown

---

1. https://books2read.com/u/3LV7ZM

2. https://books2read.com/u/3LV7ZM

together, the sparks can't help but fly, despite their efforts to resist.

Pretty soon Ava, Mario, and Harper are in a very weird, very uncomfortable love triangle that is a ticking time bomb waiting to explode. And when it does, the damage may be irreparable.

Read more at https://www.jessicaterry.com/.

Also by Jessica Terry

Love Intolerant

Watch for more at https://www.jessicaterry.com/.

About the Author

Jessica Terry caught the writing bug at a young age and loves little more than holing up at home in Douglasville, GA, cranking out contemporary novels. And eating.

Another thing she loves is interacting with her readers. Sign up for her email list and keep up to date with new releases at www.jessicaterry.com.

Read more at https://www.jessicaterry.com/.

www.ingramcontent.com/pod-product-compliance
Lightning Source LLC
Chambersburg PA
CBHW022033240626
47154CB00007B/2384